RK

Somewhere in her memory she knew she'd mad...

But was it with ... ow? If so, how coul...

D0462110

"You have to go ... ok at her. "I thought you'd be safe here, where I could watch you. Where you could tell me if you remembered anything. But now I can't guarantee that I can protect you anymore."

Last night he'd thought she should stay. This afternoon he was sending her away. Only one thing had changed in the intervening hours. They'd kissed. If only she could remember what had come between them before. Only, she couldn't. All she knew was that the taste of him was still on her lips and that she wanted to kiss him again so badly, she ached.

"I'm staying, Clint. Until everything is settled. Until you catch the killer. Until I remember what happened."

"You might be making a big mistake."

She moved closer to him, near enough to inhale the musky scent of him. "It probably won't be my first."

Dear Reader,

When actions of the past come home to haunt Senator James Marshall McCord, Texas rancher and recipient of the Congressional Medal of Honor, he knows he must protect the people he loves most in the world: his family. But he'll need some help from three very rugged, very determined men.

Harlequin Intrigue is proud to bring together three of your favorite authors in a *new* miniseries: THE McCORD FAMILY COUNTDOWN.

Starting in October 1999, get swept away by a mysterious bodyguard in #533 *Stolen Moments* by B.J. Daniels. Then meet the sexy town sheriff in #537 *Memories at Midnight* by Joanna Wayne. And finally, feel safe in the strong arms of a tough city cop in #541 *Each Precious Hour* by Gayle Wilson.

In a race against time, only love can save them. Don't miss a minute!

Enjoy,

Denise O'Sullivan
Associate Senior Editor
Harlequin Books
300 East 42nd Street
New York, NY 10017

Memories at Midnight
Joanna Wayne

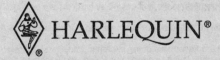

HARLEQUIN®

TORONTO • NEW YORK • LONDON
AMSTERDAM • PARIS • SYDNEY • HAMBURG
STOCKHOLM • ATHENS • TOKYO • MILAN • MADRID
PRAGUE • WARSAW • BUDAPEST • AUCKLAND

ISBN 0-373-22537-7

MEMORIES AT MIDNIGHT

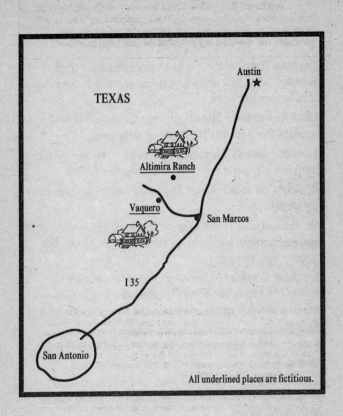

Austin

TEXAS

Altimira Ranch

Vaquero

San Marcos

I 35

San Antonio

All underlined places are fictitious.

CAST OF CHARACTERS

Darlene Remington — FBI agent and friend of Senator McCord. Her loyalty to an old friend has a killer on her trail.

Clint Richards — Sheriff of Star County. He will protect the woman he loves at any cost.

Senator James Marshall McCord — An American hero with a past that may destroy his future.

Randy Franklin — Clint Richards's deputy, but can he be trusted?

Dr. Bennigan — He's known Darlene for years, and insists he only wants to protect her and help her regain her memory.

Freddie Caulder — Senator McCord's ranch foreman. He is an expert cattleman but has his problems with other members of the senator's staff.

Jeff Bledsoe — Retired Texas Ranger and an old friend of the senator. He knows more than he is telling.

Bernie Cullen — Senator McCord's bodyguard. A giant of a man who seems totally out of place in Vaquero, Texas.

Thornton Roberts — One of the best security men in the business, he was hired to make sure the senator's ranch is always safe from human predators.

ABOUT THE AUTHOR

Joanna Wayne lives with her husband just a few miles from steamy, exciting New Orleans, but her home is the perfect writer's hideaway. A lazy bayou, complete with graceful herons, colorful wood ducks and an occasional alligator, winds just below her back garden. When not creating tales of spine-tingling suspense and heartwarming romance, she enjoys reading, golfing or playing with her grandchildren, and, of course, researching and plotting her next novel. Taking the heroine and hero from danger to enduring love and happy-ever-after is all in a day's work for her, and who could complain about a day like that?

Books by Joanna Wayne

HARLEQUIN INTRIGUE
288—DEEP IN THE BAYOU
339—BEHIND THE MASK
389—EXTREME HEAT
444—FAMILY TIES
471—JODIE'S LITTLE SECRETS
495—ALL I WANT FOR CHRISTMAS
505—LONE STAR LAWMAN
537—MEMORIES AT MIDNIGHT

Don't miss any of our special offers. Write to us at the following address for information on our newest releases.

Harlequin Reader Service
U.S.: 3010 Walden Ave., P.O. Box 1325, Buffalo, NY 14269
Canadian: P.O. Box 609, Fort Erie, Ont. L2A 5X3

Much appreciation to my sisters
Mary, Barbara, Linda and Brenda
for their unfailing support and encouragement.
A special word of thanks to
B.J. Daniels and Gayle Wilson for making
THE McCORD FAMILY COUNTDOWN
project so much fun to work on. And to Wayne,
always, for keeping the romance in my life.

Prologue

The moonless night was quiet, almost eerily so. Even the incessant Texas wind had ceased to blow. The calm before the storm.

Darlene Remington shifted in the passenger seat of the parked pickup truck, her insides quaking in spite of the months of training that were supposed to ensure that she stayed calm in any situation.

But she had known Senator James Marshall McCord all her life, and she had never seen him like this. She'd heard that he had his secret side, that if you pushed him too far, he could break you with a look. Been told that he could tear a man apart with his bare hands. But those were only old war stories, the kind that always accompanied heroes when they marched home from battle.

She turned and stared at his profile, at the bulging vein that ran the length of his neck. Whatever was eating at him had stolen his boisterous laugh and reassuring eyes. Of course, she'd known it had to be serious when he'd called Washington and asked her to fly to Texas to see him—unofficially and in private. And now he had driven her to this isolated wooded area to talk.

"When are you going to tell me what this is about, Senator?"

"I guess now's as good a time as any, if I could just figure out how to say this."

"I never thought I'd see you speechless." Her attempt at humor died before it began, another victim of the ominous darkness that encompassed them.

"What do you know about my past, Darlene? About what happened in Vietnam?"

"Mostly what's been glorified in the media. That you received the Congressional Medal of Honor for bravery under fire. That the men who served in your unit think you're just a notch under God."

"That's one side of the coin. The other isn't nearly so flattering." Reluctance and bitterness strained his voice.

"Why are you telling me this, Senator? Your past is not under investigation. At least not that I know of."

"Because my past is about to explode into the present." He reached over and patted her hand. "I hate to drag you into this."

"I'm not afraid, Senator, and you know I'd like to help you if I can." She smoothed the fabric of her denim skirt, surprised to find herself nervous around McCord. She couldn't remember ever having been before. She decided to set the parameters of the discussion up front, to avoid any misconceptions. "You know, of course, that I can't do anything that would misuse my power as an FBI agent."

"I would never ask you to." He exhaled sharply and rapped a fist on the steering wheel of the truck. "Let's get out of the truck for a minute, stretch our legs and catch a breath of fresh air."

Darlene opened her door and stepped onto the carpet of grass and dry leaves. Something stirred in the brush behind them and she strained to make out the source. Nothing moved in her line of vision.

"One of the Hill Country's many nocturnal creatures," the senator assured her, alert to the same rustling movement she'd noticed. He scanned the area and then reached back into his pickup, pulling a pistol from beneath the seat before he slammed the truck door behind him.

"You're not expecting trouble tonight, are you? If we are, this is not the best location for this discussion."

"Not tonight—but I am expecting trouble."

"More of the millennium fever that's stalking the world?"

"No. More like the ghost of years past rattling a few chains in my face."

"This is the season." She leaned against the hood of the truck, resting the heel of one booted foot on the front bumper. "It's hard to believe Christmas will be here in two weeks and after that the infamous beginning of a year that ends in double zero."

"Yes, it's strange the effect those particular numbers have on the mood of the public." Shrugging out of his jacket, he threw it across the hood of the truck and then hopped onto the right bumper. He sat, half facing her but at an angle so that his prosthetic leg dangled over the front of the truck.

"But I take it the millennium is not what you wanted to talk about when you asked me to come to Vaquero?"

"No." He reached behind him and pulled a pipe from the pocket of his jacket. "Do you mind?" he asked, tamping down the tobacco with the edge of his thumb. "I don't indulge often, but tonight I need the comfort of an old habit."

The somberness of his mood, the avoidance techniques, the need for the stem of a pipe between his lips. All so foreign to the senator's usual commanding demeanor.

Apprehension nipped at her practiced control. "Why don't you just tell me what's bothering you, Senator? That way we'll know if I can help you unofficially, or if you need to deal with this more aggressively."

"Okay, all I ask is that you hear me out to the end. Then feel free to say no to the favor I'm going to ask of you."

"I'll never say no to you if there's any way I can avoid it—not after all you've done for me. Getting me the scholarship to the university, even recommending me for the spot at Quantico."

"That's what I'm counting on."

McCord took a long drag on the pipe and exhaled slowly. When the last of the smoke had cleared his face, he began a sordid saga that grew more bizarre by the minute. Darlene sat without moving until her heart beat so painfully in her chest that she thought it might explode.

"Please stop, Senator McCord." She turned her gaze to the ground, not willing to look into his eyes. "I don't need to hear this. I don't want to hear it."

"It's too late to stop now. You have to know all of this if you're to understand why I had to take these actions."

She jerked her head up as something crashed through the bushes behind them. The sound of gunfire shattered the night, and she stared in horror at the blood that spattered her shirt.

She jumped from the side of the truck, her mind screaming orders her body couldn't seem to heed. A second later, something pounded against her head. She sank to the ground, and all she could see or feel was a suffocating blanket of black.

Chapter One

Using the toe of his right boot as a wedge, Clint Richards nudged until his left boot clattered to the wooden floor of the spacious den of the ranch house he'd built himself. Home at last, but not as early as he'd liked to have been here.

His workday had stretched into the early hours of evening, robbing him of the opportunity to take care of his own after-hour chores around the ranch. Not that he would have minded if any of the day's emergencies had been genuine, but fences cut by a couple of high-school pranksters and a neighbor's pig rooting in Mrs. Cranston's flower bed didn't warrant the kind of hullabaloo they'd produced.

And then there had been the call from James McCord. Clint had rushed over, jumping to his beck and call just like everyone else in town did. His knee-jerk reaction to the senator's call balled in Clint's gut, adding extra force to the task of removing his right boot. The boot hit the floor with such a racket that even old Loopy opened one eye and gave his master a suspicious look before thumping his tail against the hearth and returning to dog dreamland.

Clint leaned back and propped his stocking feet on the

pine coffee table before biting into the hunk of brisket he'd sandwiched between two slices of bread. Still, thoughts of McCord's call cantered around in his mind.

Good old James McCord, everybody's hero, gearing up to march from the Senate to the White House. Man of the people. But there would be at least one vote in Texas he wouldn't get.

But then, canvassing for support surely hadn't been the reason McCord had called him today and asked him to stop by. No, McCord had reasons for everything he did. This was the second time in a matter of weeks he had requested that Clint drop by with no more than a lame excuse. Well, whatever his game was, Clint wasn't interested in playing.

He reached for the remote control and clicked on the TV, surfing a few channels and finally settling for some network's version of a news show. He wasn't much of a TV man unless the Cowboys were playing, but anything would beat wasting his time thinking about the good senator.

The phone jangled beside him. He swallowed a bite of sandwich and grabbed for the receiver. "Sheriff Richards here."

"I'm glad I caught you."

Clint recognized the voice immediately. The man behind it owned and operated Jingling Spurs, one of the big-draw dude ranches just out of Vaquero. "What can I do for you, Barry?"

"We've got a little problem out on Glenn Road, just before the turnoff to my place."

"Yeah. I'm listening."

"One of my guests just drove back from town. She said a woman wandered onto the road like a wounded animal. She only caught a glimpse of her, but she thought the woman was bloody-looking. She came so close to hitting her, it scared her half to death.''

"Did she stop and check it out?"

"Yeah. But by the time she got back to the spot where she'd seen the woman, no one was there. I figured you'd want to look into it.''

"You figured right.'' Clint was already stuffing his feet back into his boots as he questioned Barry Jackson further on the details, trying to pin down the exact location that the woman had been spotted. His fatigue drowned in the spurt of adrenaline that coursed his veins as he rushed to his pickup.

The Jingling Spurs was out a long, lonely stretch of highway, and no place for a woman on foot, dazed or otherwise. Possibilities struck his mind like a nest of hissing rattlesnakes. He made a mental note to remind himself never to complain about boring, routine days again.

Grabbing a light jacket from the hook by the door and his gray-felt Stetson from the shelf above it, he stamped out the back door, glad he'd insisted that the county furnish him with a truck instead of a squad car like the city boys drove. The truck got him to places the low-riding town units could never go. Like the woods off Glenn Road.

Jumping into the front seat, Clint headed out to find who knew what, on a night so dark that the threatening rain would have trouble finding the ground—if it ever got brave enough to fall.

CLINT SLOWED HIS TRUCK to a crawl and turned on his spotlight. He searched for any sign of movement in the fenced pasture on one side of the road, and in the clumps of evergreens and scrubby brush on the other. A pair of does darted to the left of him, but other than that the black night was still.

He eased down the road, sticking to the shoulder, his spotlight emergency lights moving continuously as he scanned the area. One lone, bleeding and dazed woman was wandering somewhere in the blackness. Before he went home tonight, he'd know why, or at least see that she was safe. It was likely to be a long night.

The minutes stretched into almost an hour, and the rush of adrenaline that had fueled him earlier wore off a little more with each roll of his tires. If the woman was out there looking to be saved, she should be responding to the sound of his truck engine or the beam of police lights. *If* she was still out there and conscious.

He pulled into a dirt drive. Might as well turn around and retrace the mile he'd just covered. The rest of the area between here and the entrance to the Jingling Spurs was nothing but cleared pastureland, and the report had been that the woman had stepped out of a wooded area.

The blue lights ricocheted off metal. He turned and tried to find the source of the gleam again, but he'd lost it. Jumping from the driver's seat, he grabbed his searchlight and flooded the area with the powerful beam.

His eyes hadn't deceived him. There was a pickup truck parked not forty yards from the road, all but hidden by a stand of young pine trees.

"Anybody out there?"

The only answer to his call was the hooting of an owl overhead and the howling of a coyote in the distance. Clint's hand settled on the butt of his pistol, his feet shuffling the dry leaves under his feet and crunching them into the dry earth. Likely an abandoned vehicle, but this was not a time to leave possibilities unchecked.

He made his way to the truck, listening for any sound

of movement. Close enough now to see the full outline, he knew the pickup hadn't been abandoned for lack of value. The truck was black, expensive, the new millennium model. Just like the one McCord had been driving around town for the last couple of weeks. Apprehension stretched Clint's control, and his finger coddled the trigger of his .44. What could McCord be doing out here and why—

A weak moan killed his speculation. He spun around in time to see a woman step from the bushes and slump to the ground. He crossed the ground between them, gun drawn. The woman's clothes were torn and wet with blood, and it wasn't likely she'd done that to herself. Meaning someone else might still be lurking behind any tree.

He stooped, getting down to her level, yet keenly aware of everything about him. "I'm not going to hurt you, miss. I just need you to tell me what happened."

She shook her head, never looking up, but her hands trembled as she pulled a light jacket tighter around her chest.

"Who hurt you?" Clint leaned closer and tilted her face so that he could look into her eyes. "Darlene." The name shook from his lips, and his stomach rocked violently.

She stared at him through frightened eyes, and without thinking, he wrapped his arms about her and hugged her to him. She went limp in his arms, and for one horrible moment he thought she might have stopped breathing. For one awful instant, his own heart and lungs ceased to function. But she moved again and struggled to push away from him.

He released his hold on her. Even hurt and in danger, she wanted no part of him.

"I'm just trying to help," he said, his voice more in control than his emotions. Gingerly, he pushed back strands of blood-matted hair and examined the wound on her head. There was a knot the size of Texas, and a gash that dipped over her left eye.

"Does anything hurt besides your head?" he asked, checking her pulse.

She shook her head. Wincing, she cradled her head in her right palm. "Just my head, I think. Where am I?"

"On Glenn Road. But we're getting out of here." He lifted her in his arms and started toward his truck. She was light, and even through her skirt and jacket he could tell she was still way too thin. "Want to tell me who did this to you?"

"I...I can't." Her voice was weak, unsteady.

He let her answer ride, but he suspected *won't* would have been a far more accurate word choice than *can't*.

He trekked the path back to his own truck and settled her gently into the passenger seat, so as not to start the wound bleeding again. She moaned softly, and he clenched his hands into fists, wishing he had a woman-beating man to plow them into.

"We'll be at the hospital in a few minutes," he said, striving for a reassuring tone. "The doctor will check out that head wound and give you something for the pain."

Jerking the car into gear, he jammed his foot down hard on the accelerator and attacked the night with his flashing lights and screaming siren. No need to call for an ambulance. He could make better time. Clutching his radio phone, he contacted the hospital, letting them know he was bringing in a victim with a trauma to the head.

A victim. The word tasted metallic on his tongue. He reached across the seat and clasped her hand in his. It was cold, almost lifeless. He squeezed it gently, fighting the emotion that stormed inside him. For all the promises he'd made himself, he knew that the years that had passed had changed nothing between them.

FEAR SWAM THROUGH her mind, shaking her awake in a cold sweat of panic. She opened her eyes and looked around. The walls were dark and shadowy, lit only by the dim glow of a light above her bed. Her head was pounding, and there was an ache in her left arm.

She tried to touch trembling fingers to her head. They scraped the rough edge of a turban. *Bandages.* But where was she, and who had applied them?

"About time you woke up."

The male voice cut through the quiet. She tried to swallow past the wad of dryness that clogged her throat and burned the back of her mouth. "Where am I?"

"In the hospital. Don't you remember my bringing you here?"

She circled the room with her gaze and then brought it back to the man standing over her. He looked rumpled, unshaven, worried. She ran her tongue over her scratchy lips while she tried to make sense of her surroundings. The fog didn't lift from her mind. "Could I have a drink of water?"

"Coming right up." The man poured water from a pitcher on her bedside table. He tucked a hand under her neck and lifted her head from the bed as he held the glass to her lips. "Slow and easy. You've had a rough night, thanks to the man—or men—you tangoed with."

"Tangoed?"

"Sorry. Cop talk. Someone banged you over the head real good."

"That explains the bandage." She touched her fingers again to the gauzy turban.

The man resettled the water glass on the table, and let his fingers rest on her pillow. "Dr. Bennigan must have given you some great drugs. Feel no pain, remember no evil."

She twisted in the bed, trying to scoot up a little higher. The move sent new spasms of pain shooting through her head. "The drugs aren't as good as you think," she said, fighting back a moan.

"Then you should be alert enough to give me a few details. What happened out on Glenn Road last night?"

She searched her mind for the details he requested. Her search came up empty. "I wish I could tell you."

The man stared at her, intimidation pulsing from every muscle. Fear trembled along her nerve endings, culminating in a new series of jagged darts of pain in her head.

"Look, Darlene, don't pull that FBI secrecy routine on me. You're playing in my backyard. I deserve explanations. Especially since your buddy isn't here to answer my questions."

Darlene. The name skirted the corners of confusion that clouded her mind. This man thought she was someone named "Darlene" and that she had something to do with the FBI, but she was just...

Just who? *The drugs.* That had to be it. The man said the doctor had given her drugs. That's why she couldn't remember anything. That's why the fog wouldn't lift.

"Who are you?" she asked, straining to focus on the man and to concentrate on his answer. She could be in trouble, and she needed to get a handle on things quickly.

"Who *am* I?" He stared at her, his brows peaked. "You know damn good and well who I am. Don't put me on, Darlene. I don't know who you're trying to protect, but I'm not about to play dangerous guessing games with you."

The man was insistent, apparently used to calling the shots. She stared him down. Her bravado was false, but it was the only shield she had. "You didn't answer my question. Who are you, and why are you in my hospital room?"

Concern flickered in his steely gray eyes as he backed away from her bed. "I'll get the doctor," he said, his voice edgy, his hands clasping the brim of a cowboy hat as if it might fly away at any time.

"Wait. Do I know you?"

"You did once."

Before she could ask more, he'd all but run out the door, leaving her alone with a million unanswered questions.

Someone had hit her. She tried to think, to piece together facts. Her head spun with the questions and with new pain, but the fog only grew thicker.

The drugs. It had to be the drugs. They'd wear off soon, and she'd be her old self—whoever her old self was. In the meantime, she had to hope whoever had worked her over last night wasn't planning on a return engagement. If he showed up again, she wouldn't even know enough to call for help.

CLINT PACED THE HOSPITAL HALL. Dr. Bennigan and the staff neurologist had both examined Darlene and come up with the same diagnosis. Temporary amnesia brought on by trauma to the head.

Amnesia—the fodder of soap operas and novels. Of course, Clint had heard of amnesia occurring in real life, but he'd never encountered a true case, though he'd had several run-ins with the fake variety. Criminals were frequently experts at pretending they didn't know or couldn't recall.

But Darlene Remington was no criminal. She was an agent with the FBI. She'd been found beaten on a deserted road, and the only clue to what had happened was the truck he'd found parked nearby. A truck belonging to Senator McCord.

Senator McCord was like a father to her, she'd always claimed. Only why were she and the senator parked on a dark road in his truck? The setting seemed a little isolated for a fatherly chat. The obvious possibility ground in Clint's gut. Darlene and the senator. Parked on a lonely road. Intimate.

Acid pooled in his gut. He had to quit thinking like this. No matter what Darlene did with her life, it wasn't his concern. Not anymore.

His job was to find out what had happened last night. He'd had no luck contacting McCord, but a license check had proved the truck in the woods was his.

A senator who was on the fast track to becoming the next president of the United States, and a female FBI agent found near his truck with an amnesia-producing wound to the head. Clint had about as much chance of keeping this story under wraps as he did of stopping old ranchers from spitting tobacco on the streets of Vaquero.

Worse, somewhere out there, the man who attacked and almost killed Darlene would be walking around, probably waiting for his next opportunity. Which meant he'd have to work with Darlene, find a way to make her remember what happened last night. In the meantime, he'd have to keep her safe.

Even the thought of working with Darlene filled him with dread. If he had his druthers, he'd walk away from this case—leave it to someone with less to lose. But he'd never walk away. He was a lawman first, a man second.

Funny, that was one of the several accusations Darlene

had hurled at him when she'd told him she was leaving him to seek a career of her own, one a long way from Vaquero, Texas.

Now she was back. Only this time it was the lawman she needed.

Chapter Two

"It looks like two distinct sets of footprints to me, Clint, not counting the petite ones that match the riding boots Darlene Remington was wearing." Randy Franklin stuck his thumbs in his belt loops and studied the pattern of clues in the dirt, the piece of spearmint-scented chewing gum in his mouth taking a vigorous beating.

"Yeah." Clint made a few more notes in his ever-ready pocket notebook. "One pair of western boots and one set of prints that looks like rubber-soled sports shoes."

"The western boot prints could be McCord's. I've never seen him in anything else, though I 'spect he has some fancy street shoes to prance around in at those Washington high-society functions."

"We don't know for sure yet that McCord was even out here."

"No, but we know his truck was. And that aide-slash-bodyguard who follows him around like a deranged Doberman is making some pretty flimsy excuses as to why the senator hasn't responded to your request to come in for questioning."

Clint stooped to examine a trail of footprints and broken grass blades that led into the bushes. "Still, all we have is speculation regarding McCord."

"Geez! If I didn't know better I'd think you were trying to protect the senator." Randy scratched a spot over his left ear and hitched up his khaki trousers so that they rode a little higher over his lean hips. "What do you make of all this?"

Clint considered his response. He had a few ideas, but he wasn't ready to share them with his deputy yet. Especially with most of them so far-fetched that he was having trouble giving them much credence himself in the bright light of the morning after.

"No clear indications," he said, sticking to the bare truth.

Clint aimed his camera at a bloody rock and snapped the shutter. A rock big enough and the right shape to have cracked the top of Darlene's head, and sharp enough to have caused the gash.

He took a couple more color shots to get the location documented before packing the rock in plastic. He needed to gather all the information he could—and fast, before the place crawled with unauthorized snoopers.

"Do you think all this blood was from Darlene's head wound?" Randy stooped and pointed at a pattern of bloodstains that led back and forth from the truck into the brush. "If it is, she must have been walking in circles."

"That's entirely possible. I found her right near that scrawny pine over there." Clint motioned to the tree. "She was dazed and dragging, but, like I said, some woman saw her at the side of the road before that."

"Might have been another bloody woman they saw. Who knows what really went on out here last night?"

"No one, at this point, but the other footprints appear

to belong to men. My guess is Darlene was running away from someone. She got turned around and ended up back here where she'd started.''

"So you think it could all be her blood."

"We'll know soon enough. I called for a forensics team out of San Antonio. They'll lift the prints from the truck and take blood samples.''

"That's a little extreme, isn't it? I mean, investigations like that are usually reserved for murder cases.''

Clint batted at a gnat that was courting his eyebrows. "An injured FBI agent found in a U.S. senator's truck. One who can't remember how she was attacked or by whom. That's extreme enough for me.''

"Yeah.'' Randy rocked back on his boots. "And more than enough to rock the news-starved media.''

"If the story breaks. Which it won't, if I have anything to say about it.'' Clint slid his camera back into the pouch he had slung over his shoulder.

"Do you buy that amnesia story, Clint? It sounds a little too convenient to me.''

"The doctors appear to buy it. I'm withholding judgment until I have a few more facts.''

"Like whether or not the senator is really involved in all of this. And what he and Miss Remington were doing out here five miles past nowhere in the pitch-dark?'' Randy kicked at a bare root with the toe of his boot. "Of course, the senator's not married and neither is Darlene Remington. He wouldn't be the first man to succumb to the charms of a sexy lady half his age.''

Clint swallowed hard, angry at Randy for saying out loud what already plagued his own mind. Still, assumptions like that weren't fair to either Darlene or McCord. "There are legitimate reasons the two of them could have been together.''

Randy's gaze focused on Clint. "Legitimate reasons for a man and a woman to be having a secret rendezvous in the woods. Such as?"

Clint thrust one finger against the upper edge of McCord's truck door and shoved it, as always careful to avoid destroying any prints that might be on the handle. "Darlene works with the FBI, and McCord's got lots of political irons in the fire, and, no doubt, his share of enemies. There are plenty of reasons for them to be working together." His voice took on a sterner edge than he'd intended.

Randy didn't miss the intonation. "Hey, I'm not throwing stones. The woman's a looker—that's all I'm saying. And hanky-panky is not a crime in this county or any others in Texas that I know of."

Clint tugged his Stetson low over his forehead. "Okay, let's just drop it. The truth is, I don't know what they were doing and I don't care. Not unless it affects the investigation."

Randy stared at Clint, his eyes narrow slits in the bright morning sun. "Geez! I almost forgot. You used to date Darlene yourself before she took off for Quantico. You're not still nursing a thing for her, are you?"

"A thing? You've got to work on building your vocabulary, Randy. But don't worry. I barely remember her." His conscience balked at the enormity of the lie he'd just told. He barely remembered her the same way he barely remembered food or sleep.

Clint walked off, following a trail of blood that led down to the creek, his mind whirling. Last night he'd been too concerned with getting Darlene to the hospital to investigate fully. Besides, last night he'd thought Darlene would be able to explain what had happened out

here as soon as she recovered enough to give him answers.

And last night he didn't know that James Marshall
McCord and Darlene had left McCord's ranch together
in his fancy new pickup. Now both his bodyguard and
his ranch foreman were making excuses as to why the
man couldn't talk to Clint.

Clint's guess was that McCord wasn't around to talk.
So where was he?

"Hey, Clint. Come over here a minute. I found something."

Clint turned toward the sound of Randy's voice and
started walking in that direction, knocking the low
branches of a tree out of his way as he went. "What is
it?" he asked, talking to his deputy's stooped back.

"A wallet." Randy opened the bill compartment and
held it up. "It's been picked clean. No identification,
credit cards or photos left, either."

"Just our luck."

"Not as bad as it sounds. The leather's engraved. Take
a look." Holding the corners between two fingers, he
handed the wallet to Clint.

Clint studied the mark. McCord's brand, engraved in
the leather the way the larger version was in the tough
hide of the senator's cattle on his Altamira ranch.

"I guess we can pretty well rule out the possibility
that McCord's truck came here last night without him,"
Randy said.

"Looks like."

"A man don't leave his wallet behind if he has any
say-so in the matter. This is big, Clint."

"Yeah. Real big." Clint pulled another plastic bag
from his pocket and dropped the wallet inside. He'd been
searching for a find like this and dreading it all at the

same time. The stakes had just taken a gigantic leap. The senator might well be kidnapped or…

Or dead.

And Darlene, confused and vulnerable in a hospital bed in town might well be the only witness. His muscles tightened, and he tasted the bitter edge of fear. He pushed it aside. He had a guard at her door. She'd be safe.

"Keep looking, Randy. I'll be back as soon as I make a call from the truck."

"Anxious to report our find?"

"Yeah." And even more anxious to check on Darlene. But the deputy didn't have to know everything. A man couldn't help how he felt, but he could control his actions. He wasn't about to let the whole town know that the woman who'd dumped him years ago still messed with his mind.

He headed back to the truck, his brain shifting into overdrive. Right now he'd give a month's pay to know what had happened out here last night, and exactly what role FBI agent Darlene Remington had played.

OPEN YOUR EYES. *Open your eyes.*

She did, but still the darkness closed in, a suffocating cloak of nothingness, pushing her deeper and deeper. She flung her arms wildly. She had to grab the edge, hold on to something, anything to break her fall.

"You're all right. I'm right here with you."

Slowly the hazy brightness of reality swallowed the darkness. Darlene steadied her breathing and studied the face of the woman standing over her. Her cheeks were pudgy and red, her eyes a cool gray. But the touch was reassuring.

"Do you know where you are?"

Darlene blinked and reached to her head, letting her

fingers find and trace the edges of the familiar bandage. "In the hospital," she answered, her mouth so dry the words seemed to get stuck in her throat. "Somewhere in Texas."

"That's right. Vaquero, Texas. Is that all you remember?"

Darlene looked around the room. The lines in the curtains were sharp and clear, the furniture solid. It was her mind that held the shadows. "There was a man here." She forced herself to concentrate. "He said I'd been attacked," she continued haltingly. "That he'd found me in the woods."

"Good. That man was Sheriff Clint Richards. If you were so far gone you didn't remember him, I'd fear there was no hope for you. He's not the kind we women forget." She chuckled and fluffed her permed hair.

"I remember seeing the doctor too." Darlene scooted up, using her elbows to propel her to a near sitting position. "Was that this morning?"

"A few hours ago. You've been asleep."

Asleep. In a hospital. With her head spinning in a fog so thick she couldn't find herself. "What type of drugs am I taking? They seem to have shut down my memory."

"I'll let the doctor explain all that to you. He asked me to call him the minute you woke up. While I'm doing that, why don't you just try to relax and maybe eat some of your lunch."

The nurse pushed the swing-tray table over so that a plate of unappetizing food stared up at Darlene. "If you need anything before the doctor gets here, just buzz."

Darlene watched her walk away, the broad hips swinging beneath the crisp white of her uniform, her white oxfords silent on the tiled floor. For a second the urge to call her back was almost overpowering. Not that Darlene needed anything, but the fact that she was alone, without memory of anyone close to her, frightened her.

Instead, she picked up the packaged wet wipe and opened it, rubbing her hands with the sterile cleanser. The antiseptic smell, the slight sting to her dry hands, awakened her senses, and she realized she was hungry. Probably a very good sign, she decided. Maybe if she ate something, the food would dull the effect of the drugs.

Hands still shaky, she opened the carton of milk and peeled the paper from the plastic straw before dunking it. Actions so routine, she did them without thinking. Raising the straw to her mouth, she let the liquid spill over her tongue and down her parched throat.

The milk was cold, and she drank it all before even considering the plate of food: a slice of turkey, a helping of overcooked peas, a mound of potatoes. Funny, she recognized every item, and knew they weren't her favorites. So why couldn't she wrestle from her memory the things that mattered, like who she was or how she had ended up in this hospital? She shook her head and bit back a sob. She wasn't the type to cry.

Or was she? She might be anything—good, bad, cruel, selfish. Only, whatever she'd been had disappeared somewhere in her mind. All she knew was what the sheriff had told her. She searched her murky brain again, coming up with remnants of the morning's conversation.

Don't pull that FBI secrecy routine on me.

She had no idea what he meant, but it had been clear he didn't fully trust her. The problem was, could she trust *him?* But then, how could she trust anyone?

The door opened and she looked up, expecting the doctor and a few answers. But it was cowboy Sheriff Clint Richards who strode into her room, his western boots clacking against the tile, power and purpose emanating from his every pore.

She met his dominating gaze head-on. She might be trembling inside, but she had no intention of letting the sheriff know just how defenseless she really was. Not until she got the answers she needed from him.

CLINT WALKED OVER to the bed, the control he'd strolled in with as fleeting as morning dew in the Texas sun. It wasn't the paleness. He'd expected and prepared himself for that. It was the childlike confusion that bled into her dark eyes. It was the forced jut of her chin, the weakened condition of a woman who'd never before displayed anything but strength.

"How are you feeling?" he asked, managing to keep most of the telltale strain from his voice.

"Weak. Achy. Confused." Her lips parted in the slightest of smiles. "But thankful that I'm still alive and able to feel. In case I didn't say it earlier, I appreciate your finding me last night and getting me to the hospital."

"The best way to thank me would be to answer some questions for me, as honestly as you can."

"Then, let's make a deal. You answer mine first. Then I'll cooperate as much as I can with your investigation."

"As much as you 'can.' Do you ever talk without including qualifiers?"

"I don't know." Her voice lowered to a shaky whisper. "Why don't you tell *me?* You seem to know a lot more about me than I know about myself."

Clint pulled up a chair. Either the amnesia was genuine or she'd become much better at lying since she'd left Vaquero. "Where do you want me to start?"

"Tell me who I am. Not my name. That's written on

my wristband. Tell me who I really am, what I do, where I'm from.'' She sucked in her bottom lip. ''What kind of person I am.''

What kind of person? *The kind of woman who burrows under a man's skin, sidles into his heart, makes love with such ravenous abandonment that a man can never forget you.*

He rubbed his hands down the rough denim on his thighs. ''You're an agent for the FBI, assigned to the Washington, D.C. area, the last I heard. You joined the Bureau right after you graduated from the University of Texas six years ago.''

''Then that would make me about twenty-eight.''

''You will be on your next birthday. March sixteenth.''

''Do I have family?''

''Your father was a diplomat. He and your mom were killed in a car accident when you were a teenager. That's when you moved to Vaquero. You lived here with your grandmother during your junior and senior years in high school. After that, you went away to Austin and the University of Texas.''

''Where is my grandmother now?''

''Mrs. Remington's in a nursing home in Washington. You had her moved up there so you could be close to her.''

''Then there's no husband, no children?''

''You never married.''

''And no significant other?''

The muscles tightened in Clint's jaw, and his teeth ground together. If appearances could be trusted, last night had begun as a secret rendezvous in a parked truck that had been pulled off into the woods. A tryst with the last man in the world he'd want to think had been intimate with Darlene.

But then, he knew things about the good senator that other people didn't. And now was not the time to go into any of that. He tried to force his voice to stay steady and totally detached from the emotions that were wringing him raw.

"I guess you're the only one who can answer the question of significance in your life."

"And of course, I can't." Frustration stretched her lips into thin, drawn lines.

"The doctors say your memory will come back—that amnesia is rare, and when it occurs it is usually short-lived."

"So in the meantime, I take up residence in a hospital and wait for the man who attacked me last night to come calling again. When he does, I'll probably welcome him with open arms. He could be anyone."

"It's not likely he'll come calling here. There's an armed guard outside your door."

"An armed guard." She sucked in a deep, audible breath. "So you do believe I'm still in danger. Have you talked to the FBI? Do you know why I'm down here?"

"No, I saved that task for you. I was waiting until you were coherent enough to talk."

"I guess that's now," she said, reaching for the phone.

Clint stopped her. "I wouldn't just yet. There are a few additional facts you might like to know first."

She listened quietly while Clint replayed the few details he knew. He watched carefully for a spark of recognition when he mentioned James McCord, but the same emptiness that had haunted her eyes since the attack held tight. The only sign of emotion was the flicker of fear that caught in her voice when she questioned him in detail about the attack.

More than once he had to fight the crazy impulse to

take her in his arms. He wasn't sure if he wanted to
reassure her or just remind her that he had held her before. Only it wouldn't have reminded her of anything.
Her memories were locked away. It was his that were
getting in the way of the investigation.

He finished his slightly doctored version of the night
before and then picked up the phone. "Would you like
me to dial the Bureau for you?"

She pursed her lips in a tight curl. "So I can tell them
that I lost a senator for them and that I don't have a clue
as to where he is or who he's with? I'll be lucky if they
don't fire me over the phone. But go ahead, I might as
well get it over with. Besides, hopefully they can give us
a few clues as to what we're dealing with."

"Always the career woman."

"You say that like it's a bad thing."

"Just stating the facts, ma'am."

And facts were what he had to concentrate on right
now. A couple of important ones were that Darlene had
walked away by choice and come back into his life by
accident. Meaning, she would be walking again as soon
as her memory returned.

But first and foremost were the facts that he had a
senator missing, maybe dead, and that the perpetrator was
still on the loose. And he had every reason to come gunning for the only witness.

He dialed the number for the Washington office where
Darlene worked, and waited for the first ring before handing her the receiver. Before she'd said hello, he'd already
picked up the other phone in the room—the one he'd had
rigged to let him listen in.

She glared at him, her eyes finally reflecting the fire
he remembered so well. But she responded to the hello,

and started revealing a tale that was sure to keep the Bureau gossip lines buzzing for days.

DARLENE LAY IN THE DARKNESS of the pre-dawn hours, the night noises of the hospital finally quieting. She'd slept for a few hours, then woken to the same inky dream of falling down an endless cavity. Since then, her mind had embroiled itself with the disturbing conversation she'd had with her supervisor at the Bureau.

Apparently she'd gone into the office two days ago and asked for a few days off, vacation time that she had coming. So, whatever had brought her to Vaquero was personal, not connected to the FBI.

She turned as her door squeaked open. A man walked in, holding his hand behind his back. He pulled his hand around, and she saw the gun pointed at her and...

She tried to scream for help, but no sound came from her mouth. And then she was falling. Deeper and deeper into a cold, watery pit.

Chapter Three

Randy jumped, bouncing the front legs of his chair onto the floor as he grabbed for the knob to Darlene's door. "What's going on in here?" he demanded, rushing to keep Darlene from lunging from the bed.

Darlene sat up, her arms wrapped around her heaving chest. "Where's the man who was here?"

Randy grabbed her arm to steady her. "There's no man in here except me. The only other people who've been in here all night are the nurses who came in to check on you." He tried to keep his voice calm, though his insides weren't. He had no desire to handle a berserk female.

"But there was a man," Darlene persisted. "I saw him."

"No. You must have been having a nightmare. That's all. Look around. There's only you and me in here."

Darlene's gaze darted about the room like that of a caged animal. Finally she dropped her head back to the pillow.

"Are you all right now?"

"All right? How could I be? I don't even know reality from nightmares anymore."

"Maybe you were remembering something about how you got that lump on your head. Maybe that's what scared you. You sure looked as if you were seeing a ghost, pale-faced as you were when I walked through that door.''

She frowned. "I thought someone was in my room trying to kill me.''

"Are you sure you don't remember anything about what happened out on Glenn Road last night?"

"I'm positive.''

He slid a chair across the tile floor and placed it at the head of her bed. "I'll stay in here with you for a while. You just relax. But if you remember anything, anything at all, you tell me. Do you understand?''

"How do I know I can trust you?''

He fingered the butt on the gun at his waist. "If you can't trust the law, who can you trust?''

She rolled over on her back and stared at the ceiling. "I can't trust anyone. I *don't* trust anyone.''

He stayed in her room until she fell asleep, a fretful rest interrupted by moans and jarring jumps that seemed to affect every muscle in her body. But he was convinced now that the amnesia was real. She couldn't fake the confusion and fear that draped her eyes.

She didn't remember anything. Not yet. And she was probably all the better for it.

DARLENE YANKED at the neck of the hospital gown, pulling it down from the choking position it had assumed around her neck. She wasn't sure whether it was her role as amnesia patient or the backless, shapeless gown that delivered such a wallop of impotence when she tried to press her point with the all-knowing doctor.

This was her third morning in the hospital, and she still didn't remember a thing about the attack that put her here. Worse, last night, in spite of her insistence that she didn't want to take any more medication, she had been given another shot.

The doctor was clearly unaffected by her claims that she had never asked for the medication. And now, in the light of the sun glaring through the hospital window, even *she* wasn't sure where her nightmares ended and reality started.

She hadn't even been sure what day it was until she'd asked the nurse a few minutes ago. Thursday, December 16. She'd been here since Monday night, but it seemed more like weeks.

"I know I'm confused about a lot of things," she explained, needing desperately to make someone listen and understand her concerns. "But the last thing I remember telling the nurse was that I didn't want any sleeping medication."

Dr. Bennigan stepped toward her bed, his blue eyes studying her intently. "The confusion is to be expected, but I have your chart right here." He tapped the end of a pencil against the folder he held in his hands. "The nurse noted that you woke up fearful and asked if she could give you something to make the nightmares stop. It's documented right here."

"I don't remember that."

Dr. Bennigan smiled, his patronizing attitude rubbing her raw nerves like sandpaper. How long could she go on like this, imagining things that hadn't happened, shutting out things that had?

"Isn't it possible the nurse decided on her own that I was distraught and needed medication?"

He stepped closer to her bed, his eyes warm and friendly behind the thin wire spectacles. He was obviously trying not to upset her even more than she already was. "It's not unusual to imagine things when you're forced to deal with amnesia, Darlene. It's a very fearful state, and paranoia is not an uncommon side effect of the condition.''

She ran her thumb and forefinger along a wrinkle in her top sheet, pressing a neat crease in the cotton fabric. ''So you think I asked for the shot last night, even though I don't remember it that way?''

''I'm sure of it. You had a nightmare that left you confused, similar to the ones you've been having ever since you were admitted to the hospital.'' He placed a reassuring hand on hers. ''But I'm not surprised at your having vivid nightmares after such a brutal attack. You've been through a lot, but right now all you need to concentrate on is getting your strength back and letting that head wound heal.''

''How long do you expect that to take?''

''It's difficult to say.'' He ran his thumb down the edge of her chart. ''If we were only considering the injury, you'd be ready to leave the hospital in another day or two. Maybe even today, if you had someone with you. But—'' he scratched his clean-shaven chin and cocked his head to one side ''—the loss of memory adds another dimension to your recovery process.''

''The amnesia that we have no control over.''

''I wouldn't put it quite like that. In most cases of temporary amnesia, full memory returns within hours. Yours could return today.''

''Or never.'' The breath of exasperation escaped from Darlene's lungs in a slow stream. She was in a time warp, trapped in the present with no glimmer of the past and no confidence in her future. And lying here in this hospital bed taking mind-numbing drugs was doing nothing to aid her recall or to ease her worries. She needed to be doing something—anything—besides lying here and hallucinating about people trying to kill her.

"I'd like to check out of the hospital today," she announced, not waiting for the idea to stew too long in her muddled mind.

"Where would you go?"

"Back to Washington," she announced, faking a confidence she didn't feel. "I'd like to be in my home, surrounded by my own things. Surely that would be conducive to remembering who I am."

The doctor shook his head slowly, as if he were refusing the request of a spoiled child. "I don't think you're ready to travel, at least not until the sutures are removed. There's no major airport in Vaquero. You'd have to drive to San Antonio to even catch a flight into D.C."

"Fine. If you don't think I'm up to traveling, I'll get a motel room in Vaquero. I'll be only a few minutes from the hospital. I can come in and let you check the progress of the wound until the stitches are ready to come out. Every day, if necessary."

"So you're asking me to release you from the hospital?"

"Exactly. Is there any reason why you couldn't—?"

"Yeah. There's a very good reason." The response, authoritative and quick, did not come from the doctor.

Darlene turned to find Sheriff Clint Richards at her door, sporting an expression that dared her to argue. She ignored it.

"Do you always snoop at hospital doors?"

"I wasn't snooping, but I try not to interrupt when a doctor is conferring with his patient. I'd expect the same from the doc if I were interrogating you."

He sauntered into the room, towering above her bed

and even a head above Dr. Bennigan. He moved like a tiger, easily, yet deliberately, as if he knew what a daunting figure he made in his dark gray Stetson and pale gray western shirt. But she wouldn't be intimidated by him.

"Is that why you're here? To interrogate me?"

"Not exactly. Not at this minute, anyway."

"So why is it you think I shouldn't be released from the hospital?"

"Because I think you'd find this place a lot more hospitable than the county jail."

"Jail?" She pushed back the covers and bolted upright in the narrow bed, taking a deep breath to camouflage the surge of dizziness. "Since when did amnesia become grounds for arrest?"

"You're not under arrest. You're in protective custody."

"Funny, the way you say it, it sounds like the same thing. How long do you intend to keep me under lock and key with one of your armed guards at my door?"

"Until I find out what really happened out on Glenn Road Monday night."

Darlene fought a sudden shudder. The doctor, the nurses, the sheriff. Everyone claimed to be on her side, but they all appeared to have their own agendas.

She swung her feet over the side of the bed and dropped to the floor. Striving for steadiness, she walked the few steps to the closet, clutching the open back of her gown in a viselike grip as she maneuvered past the sheriff.

One look into the empty shelves, and her frustration swelled to dangerous proportions. "Where are my clothes?" she demanded, her voice shaky. "I know I was dressed when you found me. I do remember that much."

"And I'd probably remember if you hadn't been."

For the first time since he'd entered the room, the sheriff's lips eased into a tentative smile. The change was dramatic. It made him appear considerably more human—and dangerously attractive.

But not a tad more trustworthy.

"I'd appreciate it if someone could get my clothes for me," she said, looking pointedly from the sheriff to the doctor.

"I'm afraid that's not possible," Clint answered, meeting her accusing gaze head-on. "They're at the forensics lab being tested."

Darlene turned and leaned against the wall for support. Her missing memory was bad enough, but her instincts told her she was also being kept in the dark by the sheriff. She hated to even guess at the reason. "You are thorough, Sheriff. All this because a woman from out of town was attacked and hit over the head? Or do you think I'm involved in something besides an unprovoked assault?"

"Actually, it has more to do with your, uh, companion."

"Then I take it you haven't located Senator McCord?"

"No, but we've heard from him, at least my deputy Randy has. McCord's out of town and not available for questioning until he returns."

"Where is he?"

"That wasn't one of the answers he provided."

"But he must have told you who attacked us Monday night."

"It's obvious you've forgotten what you knew about McCord. The only thing he offered was a directive for how he expected this investigation to be handled."

"Which was?"

"He wants you to be protected at all times. Other than that, he expects the bumbling local sheriff to stay the hell out of his business and let him take care of this his way. Not a direct quote, of course.''

''I wouldn't think so.'' So that explained the hard lines that circled the sheriff's mouth and eyes, and his foul disposition. Needless to say, he had no intention of following the senator's orders. ''So where does that leave me?''

''Right here, under my 'lock and key,' as you put it, until I know what the Sam Hill is going on. Unless you can tell me what you witnessed the other night. Or unless you know where I can find the missing senator.''

''And, of course, I can't do either of those things.'' She shut the closet door and leaned against it. ''I want to go back to the area where you found me, Sheriff. It's possible I might remember what happened if I returned to the scene.''

''I don't think you should—''

She threw up her hands, interrupting the doctor. ''And *I* don't want to hear reasons from either of you as to why I shouldn't quit wasting time in this hospital room and try to get my memory back.''

The burst of determination took its toll. By the time she'd finished the ultimatum, her head was pounding and her insides were quivering. But amazingly enough, neither of the two men were shaking their heads or protesting her decision. Gathering what dignity she could, considering her state of unsteadiness and undress, she stumbled back toward the bed.

Clint pulled back the sheet. Taking her arm, he assisted her as she climbed onto the high mattress. His touch seemed almost possessive, and strangely familiar. The feeling passed quickly, and she resettled herself in the bed to gather strength for the arguments that were sure to come.

But the cowboy sheriff surprised her again. ''It sounds like your patient is anxious to leave you, Doctor.'' Clint hooked a thumb into the front pocket of his jeans and leaned against the bedside table. ''I'm willing to go with her if she's up to visiting 'the scene.'''

His nonchalant manner didn't fool Darlene for a second, not with his steely eyes burning with intensity. Returning to the area where he had found her Monday night might have been her idea, but it suited his purposes just fine.

''What do you think, Doc? Is Darlene strong enough to take a ride with me out to Glenn Road?''

Dr. Bennigan narrowed his eyes and stared Clint down. ''I told you earlier—I'm as concerned about all this as anyone. But if you try to push Darlene too hard too soon, it might backfire. In my professional judgment, she needs another day of rest.''

''That's not what she thinks. And she's the one who's fighting to regain her memory.''

Deep furrows formed in the doctor's brow. He turned to face her, his eyes mirroring his concern. ''It's against my better judgment, Darlene.''

''I'll take full responsibility,'' she assured him.

He shrugged and opened her chart. ''Well, if you're sure you're up to this.''

''I'm sure.'' She wasn't, but anything would beat lying here, worrying about what she didn't remember. Wondering what the senator was up to. Waiting to see if the attacker would return for a chance to finish her off.

''She definitely isn't ready to drive a car, and she should avoid any unnecessary stress.'' The doctor directed his statements toward the sheriff.

Clint shifted impatiently from one booted foot to the

other. "I'll take good care of her," he promised, "and have her back for bed check."

"That won't be necessary," she said, hating the way they talked about her as if she weren't there. After all, it was her memory she'd lost, not her mind. "I can get a motel room."

Neither man acknowledged her offer. Dr. Bennigan faced Clint, nodding slowly, his lips drawn as if he were agreeing to something sinister. "I guess it wouldn't hurt for her to take a ride, but don't tire her out, Clint. I know you'll be on this case night and day until you solve it, but don't try to make Darlene keep up that pace."

Clint smiled uneasily. "Hopefully, we'll put this case to bed before any of us loses any more sleep. Especially if Darlene is able to re-create for me what happened Monday night." He turned back to Darlene. "Are you ready?"

She tugged on the waist of her hospital gown. "Not dressed like this."

Clint strode back to the door and picked up a small suitcase he'd obviously left in the keeping of the guard. He set it on the foot of the bed and opened it, revealing all the necessities, including silky underwear.

"So, you had this planned all along," she said, scooting the panties out of the way and checking the size on the jeans. Size eight. Her size.

"I was hoping you were up to it."

Always move fast after a crime. The first twenty-four hours is the prime time for solving cases. The colder the crime scene gets, the less it provides. Facts. They were coming back to her. Like—

"The jeans!"

"What about them?" Clint asked, moving back toward

the bed and holding the jeans up for inspection. "They look fine to me."

"They're size eight. I wear a size eight."

"Then they'll fit." He tossed them in her direction. "We'll get out of here and let you get dressed."

"No, don't you see? When I saw they were a size eight, I knew they were my size. Automatically, without even thinking about it. That means some personal things are coming back to me, doesn't it?"

Dr. Bennigan smiled and pushed his glasses back up his nose. "I told you it's just a matter of time."

"And we don't have a lot of that." Clint pulled his Stetson low over his forehead, failing to capture a wayward lock of dark hair. "So get dressed, and we'll take a ride and see what you remember about sitting in a parked truck in the woods at night with Senator James McCord." He turned and strode from the room without waiting for a reply.

The sheriff's tone stung with accusation, and Darlene fought back a shudder as she climbed from the bed. Was the sheriff suspicious of everyone, or did he know things about her that made him doubt her innocence in all of this?

Personal business. On a dark road. With a United States senator who was now away and not talking. Darlene pulled on the jeans and stuffed her head through the yellow sweater. She prayed she would soon remember who she was. And more important, that she would like the person she turned out to be.

THE AFTERNOON SUN added a welcome sparkle to the plainness of Vaquero, Texas. Darlene looked out the truck window at the passing view, and scrutinized the parade of pickups, small houses and stores that needed paint. If she had walked these streets as a teenager, she should recall picking up the mail in the post office they'd just passed, should remember attending classes in the low, rambling high school just ahead.

Clint slowed to a stop and waited to let a lady pushing a baby stroller cross the street in front of him. Darlene stared at the diner on the corner. The sign in the window that proclaimed that Rosita's food was home-cooked and the best in town had faded to the same dull green as the clapboard building.

"Are you hungry?" Clint asked, no doubt noticing her attention to Rosita's. "If you are, we can stop and get something."

"No, I was just wondering if I'd eaten there before."

"Many times. I've never seen anyone put away Rosita's tortillas the way you can." His tone changed, grew warmer. She met his gaze, and for a second she felt she could almost reach through the haze that clouded her mind, felt that she had talked to Clint like this before. "Were we close friends, Clint?"

"Close. You might say that." He turned away from her to face the road. "Like I said, that was a long time ago. You've been gone from Vaquero for six years. A person can change a lot in six years."

He gunned the engine and turned right onto the highway that ran in front of Rosita's, but not before Darlene noticed the clench of his hands around the steering wheel and the way the fabric of his shirt stretched over the strained muscles in his broad shoulders. As always, what he left unsaid was more powerful than what he actually put into words.

"Why is it I think you don't like me very much, Sheriff? Is it something I did years ago, or just the fact that

I got myself beat up in your town and can't tell you what you want to know?''

Clint kept his gaze glued to the ribbon of highway that stretched in front of them. "Right now, I'm just trying to do my job—and that includes finding out who beat you up, and if the senator is a victim like you or if he's one of the guilty."

"You surely don't think Senator McCord attacked me!" The idea crackled in her mind, bringing up possibilities she hadn't even considered.

"It's not likely. But he may be mixed up in something that he dragged you into. Of course, we'd probably have answers to all my questions if you could remember what happened on Monday evening."

Darlene sat up ramrod straight in her seat, her blood pressure rising. "I'm really sorry that my amnesia is inconveniencing you, Sheriff. Especially since it's such fun for me."

He beat a fist against the steering wheel. "Look, I'm sorry. Okay?" His gaze left the road for the briefest of seconds, and he reached over and touched her hand. "I know this is harder on you than on anyone."

It was just a simple acknowledgment, but it was real sympathy. And it did her in. The fears and frustrations of the last few days swelled inside her, and she tried desperately to blink back the threatening tears. If she started crying now, she'd never stop. She grabbed a tissue from her pocket and dabbed at her eyes.

"Are you all right?"

She nodded, not trusting her voice.

"Look, Darlene, we don't have to do this today if you're not up to it. We don't even know if it will help."

She swallowed hard. "We *do* have to do it. For me

and for Senator McCord. If I'd done my job right the first time, this wouldn't have happened.''

''According to your supervisor, you weren't on a job.''

''Whether I was or not, I let someone attack me and a United States senator. For all we know, McCord's running in fear of his life right now. I'd say that's pretty incompetent on my part, even if the duty wasn't official.''

''I'm sure you didn't have a chance to do any more than what you did.''

''I still shouldn't have let it happen. I must have made mistakes.''

He shook his hand. ''I don't buy that.''

She stared at Clint's profile—the jut of his chin, the tight lines around his mouth. She didn't understand him at all. One minute he was cold and accusing, the next he was offering sympathy and making excuses for her.

''What makes you think I didn't make mistakes the other night?''

''You asked me how well I knew you,'' he said, his words slow and deliberate. ''I didn't give you an honest answer. I know you well enough to know that you'd never intentionally let harm come to James McCord. And you'd never let *anything* interfere with doing your job.''

''Thank you. I think.''

She leaned back in the seat, her eyes glued to the passing scenery, praying something would stimulate her brain cells and help her lost memory to kick in. But the names of the ranches tacked to swinging gates were no more meaningful than the rows of telephone poles and road signs that marched past in monotonous order.

Minutes later, she snapped to full attention as Clint pulled off the highway. He'd turned onto a dirt road that was guarded by a metal fence that swung over a cattle grate. The sign above the gate was freshly painted in large block letters: WELCOME TO THE ALTAMIRA.

"I don't understand. I thought we were going to the spot on Glenn Road where I was attacked?"

"We are. I just thought that a stop here might jog some memories. The Altamira is the McCord family ranch. You spent a lot of time here before you left for Quantico."

She sat up straighter and lowered her window. The wind had picked up, cool and heavy with the scent of new-cut hay. She looked around, struggling to remember, to find something familiar in the dirt road in front of them, the sign above the gate, the beautiful horses in the pasture to their left.

Nothing. Absolutely nothing.

"I got a call from forensics while I was waiting on you to dress," Clint said after a few minutes of silence. "It seems some of the blood on your clothes wasn't yours."

"Whose was it?"

"They're not sure yet, but it matches the type of James McCord."

The twisting and knotting started again in her stomach. She grappled with the facts she knew, trying to find meaning in the bit of news. "So, whoever attacked me must also have attacked the senator? He was probably the intended victim. We could have been led to that deserted stretch of highway you talked about, and then ambushed."

"That's possible."

"But we have no motive unless I can remember something." Frustration had her tearing at the tissue in her hand, but she wasn't about to give up. She looked through the trees and caught sight of a roofline in the distance. "Is that the McCord family home?"

"No. It was originally—back when McCord's dad was still alive. Now it serves as offices and a guard house. Security is state-of-the-art at the Altamira. You sign away everything but your first-born child just to gain the privilege of stepping inside the gate."

"Are we going to the house?"

"We won't have time this afternoon, not if we want to get to the crime scene before dark. It's a good twenty minutes from this gate to the senator's home."

She watched Clint lower the window on his side of the truck. The scents of early winter and the crispness of the air added a surreal quality to the whole maddening situation. Darlene shifted to the back of her seat. "I don't remember any of this, Sheriff. Let's just drive out to the area where you found me and the senator's truck."

He twisted the key in the ignition. "Okay, but it might help if you set the scene in your mind. Apparently you drove here Monday afternoon from the airport in San Antonio, visited for a few minutes with McCord's cook, Mary, and then got into his truck with him."

"What brought you to that conclusion?"

"You rented a car at the airport and drove it to the Altamira. The car is still there. Mary says that you had tea with her on the dining porch before you left the house with McCord."

He revved his engine and backed toward the road. "We're going to follow the same route you and McCord likely took when you left the Altamira and drove out Glenn Road."

"But why didn't we just talk at the ranch under the protection of his 'state-of-the-art' security?"

"You'll have to be the one to tell us that, since McCord's chosen not to."

"When and if I remember."

Before Clint could turn onto the highway, a cream-colored Cadillac pulled in behind him, blocking him in. A tall, attractive man, middle-aged with silvery hair, emerged from behind the wheel and walked toward them.

"Have you had any word on the whereabouts of the senator?" he asked, resting his hands on the driver's side door of Clint's truck.

"No, and we won't until he decides he wants us to."

The man stooped so that he could get a better look at Darlene. "I was sure sorry to hear you got hurt in that fray the other night, Darlene. I've told the senator a hundred times, he should be more careful now that he's a celebrity. Being a potential presidential candidate gets a man a whole lot more attention than just being a senator."

"I'm sure he'll listen next time," she said.

Both the silver-haired man and Clint laughed at her optimism.

"You definitely have amnesia if you've forgotten how stubborn McCord is," the man countered.

She sat quietly while the two men talked. She liked the older man's easy manner and the way he wasn't afraid to say the word *amnesia*. Half the hospital staff talked around it as if saying the word was paramount to condemning her to a deadly disease. Still, it was awkward meeting someone she apparently knew, and yet not having a clue who he was.

But then, she didn't even have a clue who *she* was. Her concept of herself depended solely on how others perceived her.

She wrapped her arms about her chest, fighting off a

chilling shiver in spite of the warmth of Clint's truck. In a few minutes, she'd be in the same isolated spot where Clint had found her the other night, cold and bleeding and wandering aimlessly.

Would the memories come crashing back? And if they did, would she learn facts about herself and the senator that her mind was refusing to face?

She closed her eyes. No matter what secrets lay hidden in her brain, it would be far better to know the truth than to continue living in this void.

Clint finished talking, and the man he called Thornton went back to his car. Seconds later they were back on the highway headed farther away from the town of Vaquero and the hospital.

"Was that a relative of McCord's you were talking to?"

"No, that was Thornton Roberts, the head of ranch security."

"The man in charge of the high-tech operations?"

"You got it. The man hired to keep the media from hounding McCord and his family and ranch crew night and day. Sorry I didn't introduce you. I forgot that you wouldn't remember him."

"It's okay. I was just surprised he knew about my amnesia."

"*Everyone* knows about your amnesia. Welcome back to small-town America." He took his eyes from the road to glance in her direction. "You're not having second thoughts about returning to the scene of the attack, are you?"

"Second, third and fourth," she answered truthfully. "But I don't intend to back out, if that's what you're worried about."

"Good." He slowed and turned left onto a narrow, dirt road. "Because this is Glenn Road, and we'll know in a few minutes if our little experiment is going to work."

Chapter Four

The sun was flirting with the horizon, painting the Texas sky in shimmering shades of burnt orange and pale yellow, but the gentle glow of the sun didn't lessen the sense of foreboding as Darlene pushed open her passenger door and stepped into the long, wispy grass.

As much as she longed to remember everything that had happened in this deserted spot on Monday night, she wasn't sure she was ready to discover her role in the events. If she'd been on duty, it would have made a little more sense. But as it was, she couldn't imagine what had bought her and the senator out here to talk.

The possibility that she had been used to set up McCord nagged her conscience, even though Clint seemed to think she was too much the FBI agent to ever let that happen. So, did he think she and the senator had been involved in a romantic tryst? A sexual affair that would cause McCord trouble if it were picked up by the media?

She walked away from the truck and stopped near a scraggly cedar, grappling with memories that wouldn't materialize. She never heard Clint get out of the truck, but she sensed him at her elbow and heard the reassuring rhythm of his breathing just behind her ear.

"I found you just over there." He pointed in the direction of a slender pine tree. "You stepped out of the brush and slumped to the ground, holding your head."

A chill chased through Darlene, and she hugged her arms about her waist. Clint wrapped an arm around her shoulder. "I have a jacket in the truck."

"No. It's not the temperature."

His arm tightened about her. "Is it memories?"

She rocked against him, suddenly weak, her insides jumpy. "More of a feeling than a distinct memory."

"Okay, slow and easy. Don't force it. Just let it happen."

He tugged her around to face him. She tilted her head and looked into his eyes. The intensity of his gaze was almost frightening, so invasive that she felt he could see clear through to her soul.

"What are you feeling?" he asked.

"Fear. I remember fear." The frigid chill fastened its icy fingers around her heart. "And blood. Lots of blood." She squeezed her eyes shut, but the images only grew more vivid. She strained to see through the crimson fog that filled her mind, but it was too thick. It was blinding her, the fear stealing her breath away, the same way it had done the other night in her hospital room.

Clint pulled her to him, held her tightly against his chest. "You're okay. I won't let anyone hurt you."

His voice was hoarse, but his strength wrapped around her the way his arms had. She clung to him, burying her face in the smooth fabric of his shirt. And as if by a wave of a mystical wand, nothing seemed quite as frightening as it had moments before.

"What else do you remember?" Clint urged. "Who was here with you? What happened to McCord?"

"I don't know." She sucked in a steadying gulp of

air, the force of it burning her lungs. "I remember my head aching. I remember being afraid. But the only face I see is yours. Standing over me, pulling on me."

"That was when I found you here. But it was all over by then. Think. Try to focus. What happened before I got here?"

Frustration filled her, so thick she could taste its bitterness. Clint needed her memories. They both did.

"Can you remember who attacked you?"

"Nothing." She spit the painful word out of her mouth. "I remember nothing."

He reached for her hand, but she stalked away, angry with him and even angrier with herself for wanting what she couldn't give. Her gaze circled the area, desperate to see something that might make the cold haze in her brain take form. When that didn't work, she started pacing back and forth, stopping to look at every bush, every rock, every mound of earth.

Clint kept his distance, but she felt the heat of his stare as he watched her every movement, almost willing her to break down the memory barriers that were holding her captive. As badly as he wanted to know what happened here Monday night, she was sure she wanted it a hundred times more.

To him, it was an investigation. To her, it was the sum of her life up until the moment she'd stumbled into him three nights ago.

"McCord's truck was parked just over there," Clint said, breaking the silence when she stopped to lean against the trunk of an oak tree.

She scrutinized the spot he'd pointed out. "I suppose you've had the vehicle checked for evidence."

"It's still being checked. So far, the only fingerprints

have belonged to McCord, you, or people who worked
for him.''

"You can't rule out the people who work for the senator.''

"I haven't ruled out anyone.''

"Including me.''

"No—'' he took her hand in his ''—excluding you,''
he said. He dropped her hand, and placed his on the tree
just behind her head. "You didn't do anything wrong in
all of this. So, if that's one of your worries, you can check
it off your list.''

Darlene tried to pinpoint the crazy sense of familiarity
that had washed over her at his touch, but she couldn't.
"You can't be sure of anything about me,'' she said finally. "You said so yourself. Six years is a long time. A
person can change.''

"Not that much,'' he said, then added, "It's getting
late, and I promised not to tire you. Are you ready to go
back to the hospital?''

"I don't give up that easily.'' She turned her back to
him and headed up a rocky incline. Surely, there had to
be something out here to jog her memory. She topped a
small hill and scanned the area below her. Grass, bushes,
another barb wire fence in the distance—

And a glimpse of color peeking out from a leafy bush.
Blue plaid. She closed her eyes, and the fabric took shape
in her mind. *A shirt. Splattered in blood.* She froze, determined not to let the haze block out the images before
she could make sense of them.

Perhaps someone had been wearing that shirt the other
night. If she tried hard enough, she should be able to
picture the man who wore it. But even the image of the
shirt faded in and out, like a video losing its feed. She
closed her eyes tightly, praying for the events of the other

night to release their hold on her. To let the memories she'd buried fight their way to the surface.

Blood. Evil. Secrets.

One minute she was lost in her thoughts, the next the illusions were shattered by the crack of a rifle. Instinct and training took over where reasoning failed. Screaming a warning to Clint, she dived for cover.

CLINT JERKED TO ATTENTION as the sound of Darlene's scream mingled with the explosion of rifle fire. Racing at breakneck speed, he topped the small hill where he'd last seen her. His fear mounted. There was nowhere for her to go, but she was gone.

"Darlene!" His voice echoed around him, mocking him. He should never have left her alone, should never have let her out of his sight—not here where the attack had occurred. His finger rolled across the cold metal trigger of his pistol.

"Darlene!" He didn't try to keep the panic from his voice. Scanning the area, he searched for any sign of movement, listened for any noise that might tell him where she was. Moments ago she'd been in his arms, holding on to him. Now she had disappeared into thin air.

"Clint."

He whirled toward the sound of the shaky voice. Darlene was on the ground, crawling from behind a cluster of thorny branches. Safe, except for a few scratches on her arms and chin. Relief left him weak but still wary. "What happened?"

"I heard a gunshot."

He helped her to her feet. "I forget you've become a city woman. I should have warned you it was deer season. We're overrun with hunters this time of year."

"Hunters, probably not even near here, and I dived for cover. One more example of my amnesia-produced paranoia." She brushed at the front of her jeans and picked a nettle from the denim.

"More likely the result of your training." He trailed a finger across her cheek, wiping loose strands of hair away and tucking them behind her ear. "We law-enforcement types never take gunfire lightly."

"You didn't scream and jump for cover. Besides, I don't even remember being in law enforcement. But..." She hesitated, shifting from one foot to the other.

"Say whatever you're thinking, Darlene. This isn't the time for holding back."

"I know. But this sounds hokey, even to me." She put her fingers to her temples and shook her head slowly, as if to clear away cobwebs. "I noticed that scrap of material caught in the bush just beyond that rocky area." She pointed downhill, toward a cluster of scrubby bushes and a glimpse of light blue fabric.

"For a few seconds, my mind went crazy on me. I saw someone wearing a blue-plaid shirt, one splattered with blood." She drew her bottom lip into her mouth.

Clint made his way to the scrap of fabric she'd pointed out and pulled it free. It was the end of a ripped sleeve, the cuff still intact.

He turned to find Darlene a few steps behind him. "Not nearly as hokey as you think. I stopped by McCord's place Monday afternoon. He was wearing a blue-plaid shirt. I'd say your memory is fighting to pull free."

Groaning, she touched the fabric with the tip of her finger. "Senator McCord's blood on my clothes. The shirt he was wearing ripped to shreds." She looked away from Clint and stared into nothingness. "Are you sure he's all right, Clint? Are you sure he's not dead?"

"I told you. He called the Sheriff's Office and talked to Randy."

"His voice could be faked. There's equipment that can do that, make the voice imagery so precise, it's impossible to tell the difference over the telephone." There it was again—facts she knew without a clue as to when or where she'd learned them. Like the images, they seemed to come from nowhere.

"We don't have a body, Darlene. Just a torn shirt."

"And McCord's blood on my shirt."

He took her hand and was amazed at how cold it was. "Don't jump to any conclusions. McCord is tough as nails. Believe me. He didn't get the Congressional Medal of Honor for lying down and letting trouble gallop over him."

Something moved behind them. Without stopping to think, Clint moved in front of Darlene and cleared his holster with the pistol in one quick movement. A crow swooped down from a tree and strutted in front of him. He waited to make sure the crow had been the guilty party before sliding the gun back into the holster.

"You're quick," Darlene said, eyeing the pistol. "I pity the criminal unlucky enough to have to go up against you."

"I like to be prepared."

"That, or you aren't convinced the earlier shot was just a hunter."

"Your FBI mind is showing again."

"At least you seem to think I still have a mind. You might be a majority of one. Dr. Bennigan appears to believe I'm lost in Loonyville. A paranoid amnesiac, if there is such a diagnosis. What worries me the most is that I'm beginning to agree with him."

"Don't. And don't let the doc get to you. Occasionally

he's short on tact, but he's top-notch. Caring too. We're lucky to have him in Vaquero. Small towns like ours have trouble luring and keeping good doctors.''

.''A small friendly town where everybody knows everybody else.'' She rubbed at a scratch on her hand. ''So what do you really think provoked the attack on McCord and me, Clint? You have to have a clue. You said you had been to his ranch Monday afternoon. You must be friends with the senator.''

''Friends? I wouldn't go that far. Let's just say we live in the same county.''

''Do you think he was mixed up in something shady? You hinted as much earlier.''

''I have no idea what went on here Monday night, except that someone came after you with what looks like the sharp end of a big rock, and the senator who was with you ran and took cover instead of staying around to see that you were safe. Now he's avoiding questioning.''

''Not acts to inspire trust,'' she said, her eyes reflecting the confusion that had to be weighing her down.

Clint had no trouble empathizing. *He* was confused—and his memory was intact. ''Until I find out what happened,'' he said, ''I don't trust anyone. You shouldn't either.''

''Not even you?'' she questioned, her slim, lithe body inching closer to his, her face upturned so that she could read his expression when he answered.

Old doubts settled like lead in his chest. She should trust him least of all, but not for the reasons she was thinking. He managed what he hoped was a reassuring smile. ''You can depend on me to keep you safe if the man who attacked you comes back to finish what he started.''

''Are you sure my attacker was a man?''

"The evidence points that way. There were two sets of footprints other than yours found here at the scene of the attack. The other two sets appeared to be men's. Likely McCord's and the attacker's. Of course, it is possible that the footprints belonged to a woman."

"Going on the assumption that it is a man, if he had wanted me dead, he could have killed me the other night."

"Not necessarily. He had McCord to handle. By the time he chased after him, you must have had time to get away."

He dropped a hand to her shoulder, knowing, the second he did it, that he shouldn't have. No touch between them was so impersonal that he didn't feel the pang of wanting to hold her close. He'd have to stay on guard constantly, or else be faced with the same agonizing withdrawal pains he'd suffered the last time she'd walked out of his life.

He dropped his hand from her shoulder and buried it in his front pocket. "McCord is convinced you're in danger. Which means either that he told you something that put you there or that you saw something."

She scanned the area again, as if she believed the answers lay somewhere in the grass or the trees. "If that were true, wouldn't the perp think I'd already talked to you? It would be too late to stop me from talking if that was what I had a mind to do. Unless he knows I have amnesia."

"If he's from around here, he probably heard you had amnesia before you did. I think we've stayed long enough, Darlene. If the setting were going to inspire you to remember more, it should have worked by now. It looks like the shirt is the best we're going to come away with."

She matched her pace to his and walked at his side. "Back to the hospital and another round of nightmares in which people are trying to kill me." She picked up her pace. "The subconscious does strange things, doesn't it?"

"The mind is very powerful," he said, opening the passenger door of his truck. "Sometimes it's our best weapon."

"Still, it's strange. The truth is blocked out, but terrifying untruths are as vivid as if they actually happened. I dread going to sleep anymore. I'm afraid at some level that I won't wake up."

Her uncharacteristic defenselessness hit him hard. "Would you like me to stay with you tonight? I need to stop by McCord's place later for a serious chat with his foreman, but I could come to the hospital after I leave the Altamira."

She hesitated, and then sighed. "No. Thanks for the offer, but the guard is enough. I really don't need you."

No surprise there. He'd known it for years. Still, the words pricked, and he hated the feeling. Hated the fact that six years after Darlene had dumped him, she still had the power to make him feel something.

Climbing behind the steering wheel, he started the engine and yanked the gear into reverse. He was the sheriff, Darlene was the victim and his prime witness. Nothing more.

But it would be a lot easier to remember those facts if the scent of her didn't fill the cab of his truck. If he hadn't lain awake half of every night since she'd dropped back into his life, thinking about what it had been like when she'd shared his bed.

Such stupid reactions would lead to costly mistakes

unless he could get a handle on his emotions—and fast. He could use a little amnesia himself right now.

DARLENE SETTLED BACK in her seat, unanswered questions about everything she could think of rocking her mind. Clint could possibly provide a lot of the answers, but something in the hard lines of his face told her he was consumed by the mystery at hand and wouldn't appreciate being disturbed.

Odd, though. They had apparently been good friends at one time. She'd felt a glimmer of the bond they must have shared minutes ago when he'd held her in his arms. Yet they had stopped communicating completely six years ago.

Another piece to the puzzle of her life that was lost somewhere in the depths of her subconscious. She pushed the thoughts from her mind. It was the attack, and the senator, she needed to be thinking about. If the senator wasn't dead, she had to do everything in her power to remember something that would help them locate him.

"Who are you going to talk to at the Altamira?" she asked when she could keep silent no longer.

"Some friend of McCord's who he hired to manage his ranch while he's off politicking. I've talked to him twice and gotten the runaround both times. Either he doesn't know anything, or McCord's warned him not to talk to me."

"Why don't I go with you?"

He shot her a dubious look. "Why should you? Besides, I promised Dr. Bennigan I wouldn't tire you out."

"I'm not tired. And you said yourself, I've spent lots of time at the ranch. It can't hurt to see if something there jogs my memory, and I certainly wouldn't mind missing dinner at the hospital."

"Not your D.C. gourmet food, huh?"

"Who knows? But I'll bet you a margarita it doesn't compare to Rosita's."

"Are you asking me out to dinner, FBI Agent Remington?" His eyebrows raised speculatively.

"Why not? You said it wouldn't be the first time we'd eaten together there."

He cocked his head in her direction. "Are you sure you're up to this?" Because he sure as hell wasn't.

"It's only a stop at the Altamira and dinner. Of course, I'm sure."

Clint pushed his Stetson back a little farther on his head. "Then get prepared. You're about to re-meet Freddie Caulder, one of the most cantankerous men you've ever had the displeasure of dealing with."

"Then why would McCord hire him?"

"It's said he knows his cattle six ways to Sunday. And he's McCord's friend."

"Another man I shouldn't trust?"

Clint thought about it. The man was loyal to McCord, but that probably wouldn't spill over to his friends. Only, maybe McCord didn't even trust his friends. If he did, why hadn't he returned to the ranch after the attack?

"You could trust him with your cows," Clint offered, "if you had any. Other than that, I'd add him to the list of men to watch out for."

"It's going to be a long list."

"Be thankful this is a small town."

THE HOUSEKEEPER ANSWERED the doorbell on the first ring, still wiping her hands on the skirt of a gingham apron that billowed over her plump figure.

As soon as the door swung open, she reached for Darlene, burying her in a bear hug. "I've been so upset, worrying about you," she said, hugging all the tighter. When Darlene didn't respond with the same enthusiasm, she held her at arm's length for an inspection.

"Look at you, girl. You left here the other night looking just as pert and pretty as ever. Now you're pale as a cat in the flour bin, and that bandage practically covers the left half of your head."

"It's not as bad as it looks," Darlene answered, ill-at-ease over the attention she was getting from a woman she couldn't remember.

"Don't you worry none," the garrulous woman offered as she led them into a spacious room that smelled of leather and wood fires. "The sheriff here will find the men who've done it to you, and he'll track down our Jim and help him out too. If he needs it, that is. Truth is, our Jim's probably outsmarted the rascals by now and is bringing them in for Clint."

"You've probably heard that Darlene is having trouble with her memory," Clint explained.

"You poor thing." The housekeeper turned her attention to Darlene again, patting her on the shoulder as she walked past her. "I heard you can't remember what happened on Glenn Road the other night, but surely you remember me."

She shook her head. "I'm sorry. I'm sure we were good friends, and it will all come back to me soon."

The woman didn't let it go at that, but she did switch the focus of her interrogation to Clint. "She remembers you and the senator though, doesn't she? I mean, she's known the both of you for years."

Darlene grimaced as the woman suddenly started treating her as if she could no longer understand English. "I have a temporary memory loss from the accident and the drugs," Darlene said, deciding the full spiel was preferable to being talked around. "I should be back to normal any time now."

Back to normal. Geez, she'd said it herself, admitted she wasn't normal now. Local girl turned amnesiac freak. She could hear the gossip mills grinding.

Clint formally introduced her to Mary, McCord's long-time housekeeper, cook and caretaker of his daughter until Levi had gotten big enough to care for herself. They exchanged greetings as if they were meeting for the first time, but now Mary was clearly on edge, eyeing Darlene as if she were an oddity from some traveling carnival exhibit.

Darlene took the offered seat on the leather couch and surveyed the surroundings. Clint said she'd been here many times before, in which case, the Altamira should be as familiar to her as her left foot.

The den where they sat was expansive, high-ceilinged with rough-hewn pine beams, the walls painted a light yellow, the polished wooden floor splashed with color from the woven rugs scattered like lily pads in a brown pond. A room fit for men, but still bearing a woman's touch. Maybe Mary's, she decided, since there was no wife.

The stone fireplace in front of her was mammoth, and what appeared to be the first logs of the evening were just bursting into flame. She let her gaze wander to the framed photographs that hung on the wall. All strangers.

No, not all. She recognized a younger version of herself in one of them, standing with a tall man—a beard covering his chin—and a woman close to her own age. She walked over to get a better look. A second later she felt Clint's presence behind her.

"That's you with McCord and his daughter Levi. The

bay is Whiskey. He belongs to McCord, but you rode him in some local rodeo events.''

"The barrels."

"You remember that?" Clint's tone grew deadly serious.

Darlene put her hands over her eyes, willing the image that had flashed so quickly through her mind to return. But her efforts were useless.

"No, for a second I could picture myself on the horse in the picture, riding the barrels in a rodeo, but when I tried to wring the details out of the image, it vanished." She drew inside herself, fighting the urge to cry out, to stamp her feet, to slam her fist into something. "When was the picture taken?" she asked, controlling her frustration as best she could.

"The summer you graduated from the University of Texas, just before you left for Quantico."

Clint's shoulder brushed hers as he answered, and an unexpected warmth crept through her. She trembled as a blush she couldn't understand flushed her cheeks.

"I don't know why I'm standing around shooting the breeze like I didn't know manners from moles," Mary broke in. "I've got fresh coffee already brewed, and a plate of just-baked sugar cookies."

"Not for me," Clint said. "I'm going to ring up Caulder, see if he wants to drive up here to chat or if he'd rather I come to his place."

"Humph. You won't find him anywhere about." Mary made no attempt to hide her displeasure.

"Why not?"

"He left this morning, said he had business down in San Antonio and he didn't know when he'd be back."

"That so?" Clint hooked his thumbs into the front pockets of his jeans and leaned against the door frame.

"Strange timing, don't you think? What with McCord out of pocket."

"Everything that's gone on around here lately's been strange. Ever since Thanksgiving, things have been going to hell in a handbasket. Excuse my language, Darlene, but it's the pure truth. The senator is a troubled man, and he's been plumb irritable most of the time. It's not a bit like him. Now he just up and leaves and doesn't even tell me where he's off to."

Clint strode over to the hearth, close enough to look Mary in the eye. "Did McCord say anything to you about what the problem was?"

"Not to me. You know how he is. And Freddie Caulder is just like him. They both think they can take on the world without any help from anyone, especially from the womenfolk. The same way you are, Clint, so you ought to understand what I'm talking about better than anyone."

Darlene joined the two of them in front of the fire. She had a few questions of her own that needed answers while Mary was in such a talkative mood. "Did Senator McCord call and ask me to come to the Altamira, Mary, or did I just show up?"

"He asked you to come. Not that he told me that, mind you, but I heard you question him when you walked in the door, wanting to know why he'd insisted you come to Vaquero at once."

So, she hadn't just taken a few days of vacation as she'd told her supervisor. She'd come to the ranch at McCord's request.

As soon as Mary left the room to fetch the coffee, Darlene returned to her spot on the couch and motioned for Clint to join her. "You said you had been to the

Altamira on Monday afternoon, Clint, apparently before I got here."

"Right. That's how I knew McCord was wearing the blue-plaid shirt."

"Why were you here?"

"McCord called me." Clint leaned back and crossed a booted foot over his left knee. "When I got here, he offered some lame excuse that his fence had been cut and some of his cattle were running loose."

"Isn't it possible that could have been the truth? There are miles of fences out here."

"It's possible he had his fences cut, but not that he'd be calling me about that. Like Mary said, he's a man who likes to handle his own problems."

"So you think he called you for another reason, and then decided not to tell you."

"You got it. He did the same thing Thanksgiving Day, about the time Mary said she started noticing trouble. Right after that his daughter was in some bizarre kidnapping scheme that he designed himself because some crackpot in the Northwest made a threat against her."

"This could all be tied together." For the first time since the attack, she felt like they were getting somewhere. "Where's that crackpot now?"

"Dead and buried. Shot by a co-conspirator."

"And the co-conspirator?"

"You definitely think like an investigator. But this is a dead-end trail. I've ridden it for two days myself and gotten nowhere. Both men involved in the threats and the attack on Levi were killed. But there's no shortage of crackpots out there, and the more publicity McCord draws, the more frequently he's going to be targeted by someone with an ax to grind."

"I'm surprised anyone wants to run for president."

Their conversation halted as Mary stepped back through the open door. Darlene turned down the cookies, opting to wait for Rosita's tortillas, but she savored every drop of the rich coffee, so different from the lukewarm, watered-down beverage the hospital had served with her lumpy oatmeal.

The hospital. A place of healing, yet she dreaded going back there tonight, even though the afternoon's activities had taken more out of her than she planned to admit to either Clint or the doctor. They would only see it as a reason to keep her imprisoned in that dratted room.

One more night was all she planned to stay there, with an armed guard at her door, provided by a sheriff who believed she was in imminent danger.

A sheriff whose touch affected her in strange and sensual ways that made no sense...unless they had been more than friends six years ago.

And that was one question he could answer tonight at dinner.

Chapter Five

"I love the smell of this place," Darlene said, stepping into Rosita's.

"Spices and grease?"

"That works for me. Can we grab that table by the window or do we have to wait for them to seat us?"

"This is Vaquero, Texas. If you wait to be seated, you'll go home hungry." He followed her to the table by the window, his heart twisting inside that she'd chosen it. Maybe her memory was a lot closer to the surface than she realized.

Or maybe he was giving in to wishful thinking, a pastime he should have put away with his cap guns.

He watched Darlene scan the area, her eyes lingering on first one group of diners and then another.

"Is this what you expected?" he asked, knowing from her expression that Rosita's hadn't evoked the memories she'd hoped for.

"I didn't expect it to be this crowded."

"Saturday night's strutting night. All the wranglers have to take their best girl out for dinner." He held Darlene's jacket while she shrugged out of it, and then laid it on the chair next to her, choosing the seat across from her for himself.

"So why aren't you with your best girl?" she asked, looking up at him as he pulled his chair closer to the bare Formica table.

Her green eyes were taunting him, her full red lips curled into a seductive smile. Old sensations settled into the pit of his stomach like molten metal. His mind was playing tricks on him, making him picture her the way she'd been six years ago. Youthful, flirtatious, giddy with desire. Why the devil had he brought her here?

Easy answer: poor judgment.

Now he didn't have a lot of choice but to make the best of it, and then avoid this kind of punishing behavior in the future.

"My best girl is a four-legged filly, and she doesn't cater to restaurant food," he said when he was sure his voice and libido were controlled enough not to make a fool of him. "Barley and oats are fine with her."

"I'm surprised the local ladies let you get by with that. I'd guess more than one would have her sights set on a cowboy cop with dark, curly hair and a roguish smile— that is, when he lets one slip out."

"I try to avoid women with their sights set. It keeps everyone from being disappointed." He picked up the stained menu that rested between glass shakers of salt and pepper. Not that he needed to see what it said; the offerings had changed very little in all the years he'd been coming here.

"Well, would you look at this? Darlene and Clint, together again. And I'd all but stopped believing in miracles."

Clint looked up from the menu, groaning inside. With his luck running the way it was, he should have known it would be Rosita herself who waited on them tonight.

"Lawmen have to eat too," he answered, making light

of the fact that he was having dinner with his old girl-friend, and hoping Rosita took the hint.

"You need to get your eyes checked, Sheriff, if you think that is a *lawman* sitting across from you." She took her hand from her hip and stepped closer to Darlene, bending over to get a better look at the bandage. "And I don't know what kind of police work the two of you have been doing, but it doesn't look healthy to me."

"No worse than eating your enchiladas. They've been banned by every heart surgeon in the state," he teased.

"Don't go believing all that hogwash you hear about a few fat grams. My enchiladas are good for the stomach and for the soul. Everybody needs a little fire in their belly sometimes. Now are you ready to order, Darlene, or do you want me to just bring you a plate of tortillas to munch on while you decide?"

Darlene set her menu on the edge of the table. "What are you having, Clint?"

Rosita saved him the trouble of answering. "The sher-iff here is so predictable, I usually just stick his order in for the beef enchiladas when he walks in the door."

Darlene picked up her salsa-stained menu and handed it to Rosita. "Bring me the same, only make mine chicken."

"Extra hot?"

"Sure. If the sheriff can handle the fire in his belly, I can too."

Rosita walked away laughing.

Clint didn't laugh. For two cents he'd get up right now and haul Darlene back to the hospital. He had to be out of his mind to think he could work with her as if she were just any other victim. Her memory might be shot to hell, but his was alive and bucking at the barn door.

"Clint."

Her voice dragged him out of his butt-kicking reverie. He met her gaze across the table.

"You seem so agitated. Is something wrong?"

He scooted the paper napkin from in front of him. "You mean, besides the fact that we're no closer to finding your attackers than we were three nights ago?"

"Right. I'm talking about us now. What is it about me that upsets you so much?"

"What makes you think you upset me?"

"The way you act. One minute you're friendly, but the next it's as if you can't bear to be around me."

"You're reading me wrong. I'm just doing a job. I haven't even talked to you in years, except to speak if we ran into each other when you were visiting Vaquero."

"That's another thing that puzzles me. Why haven't you seen me? I must come back to Vaquero fairly often. Rosita wasn't surprised to see me—only to see me with you. And you said yourself that I was a frequent visitor at the Altamira. If we were friends before I left, why didn't we visit when I was back home?"

Clint shifted in his seat, wishing he were anywhere but here, and talking about anything but this. If he told her the truth, it would only intensify the awkwardness between them. Not that he could tell her the truth. His ego was far too fragile to take that kind of beating. He settled for a partial truth. "Between running my ranch and being the sheriff, I don't have a lot of time for socializing."

"I think you're lying."

She reached across the table and laid her hands on top of his. He drew them away as if she'd hit him—a stupid, teenage response. After all, she was groping to recover her life. He was dodging pain that he would have sworn had died a long time ago.

"What happened to our friendship, Clint? Was it something I did?"

"I can't see a lot of sense in digging up the past right now."

"That's because you have one."

Her voice was low, tinged in frustration. He looked up into smoky eyes that almost took his breath away. "Exactly what is it you want to know about our relationship?"

"Were we lovers?"

Clint averted his gaze to the paper napkin. He could answer her in one word, but she'd never be satisfied with that. And there was no way he was going to sit in this restaurant and try to describe the relationship they'd shared that summer.

"We made love," he finally answered, his body reacting to that simple, understated response in ways that made him glad he was sitting behind a table. "We were also friends a long time before it got to that stage."

"What happened between us?"

"I guess you'd say our lives just ended up in different places. You went to Quantico to pursue your career. I stayed here in Texas, the only life-style I know how to live."

"You make it sound so matter-of-fact, so cold."

Clint picked up his glass of water and drank it down. He had half a mind to show her what it had been like between them, to throw her across his shoulder and haul her off to the barn where they'd first made love. If she wanted to give her memory a true test, he'd see if she could recall how she'd moaned in pleasure and begged for more.

He sat the glass back down with a clatter. He had to get a grip. Too much was riding on his ability to think clearly. "We were young," he said, "and what we had was no more than a summer fling."

The lie lay between them, a bitter but welcome barrier. If she bought it, it would help keep their current relationship all business.

She fingered her napkin, but didn't respond until one of the younger waitresses had set a basket of hot tortillas, a bowl of spicy dip and one frozen margarita between them. Darlene thanked the girl and took a sip of the drink before pushing it toward Clint. As much as she'd like more than a taste, she knew it wouldn't mix well with the drugs in her system.

"Then there were no hard feelings between us when we parted?" she asked, turning her attention back to Clint. "I mean, neither of us did anything cruel that would make us hate each other, did we?"

Cruel? Not unless you counted destroying his dreams and breaking his heart as cruel acts. Actually, she'd done him a favor, the same kind McCord had done him years ago: taught him not to expect anything from anyone but himself.

"We didn't have any knock-down brawls or have to cancel any wedding cake orders."

"Good." Darlene buttered a tortilla and dipped it in the bowl of hot sauce. "Then there's no reason we can't work together as fellow law enforcers now."

"That all depends. What kind of work did you have in mind?"

"First off, I think we should locate the senator. I've been thinking."

"If it's about getting involved in *my* investigation, forget it."

"Not so quick. I have an idea that could break the standstill. Suppose I act like I remember everything—that should bring my attacker out in the open. When he strikes, we'll be ready for him. The old give-'em-the-bait trick.''

''Bad idea.''

''Do you have a better one? We can't just wait around for him to attack again.''

''There is no 'we' here, Darlene. You've been relieved of duty. This is my investigation, and I haven't been 'waiting around.'''

''Ah, ah, ah.'' She put her hand up to stop his tirade. ''I'm the one with amnesia, but you have a very short memory. You just admitted there was no reason we couldn't work together, so don't get high-handed with me. Besides, I'm the one the senator called when he was in trouble, not you. And I'm the one who witnessed the attack.''

''You don't remember it.''

''But I will. Any minute now. So why not push the truth a little and get the ball rolling?'' Darlene wiped her mouth with her napkin, catching some sparkling grains of salt left by the margarita glass. ''You have to let me help,'' she insisted. ''I can't bear just sitting in that hospital feeling sorry for myself, wallowing in forgetfulness. It's not me.'' She took a deep breath and clasped her hands. ''At least, I don't think it is the real me.''

''No, not unless you've changed a whole lot. But the real me doesn't put women in danger.''

''I'm glad to know that. It gives me all the more reason to count on you and that big gun you're wearing to keep me safe.''

The conversation was interrupted by the arrival of plates of chili-covered enchiladas, Spanish rice and re-fried beans. The smoke from the hot food curled around Darlene's nose, and she sighed as she breathed in the aroma. "If it looks as good as it tastes, I may never leave Vaquero again."

And on hearing her comment, Clint's appetite departed faster than a starving bull through a busted fence.

DARLENE AND CLINT TRIED to sneak back into the hospital as quietly as possible, knowing the staff would frown on the patient returning with tequila on her breath, even though she'd only had a couple of sips. But they had the bad luck to meet Dr. Bennigan rushing out the door of her room.

The doctor whirled around and followed them in. "You need to get right back into that bed, young lady. I certainly never intended for you to be out of the hospital this long. I know Clint has no sense of restraint when it comes to working on a case, but I thought you would."

"I'm fine." But she didn't protest when Clint took her coat and led her to the bed. The activities, the food and the taste of the margarita were taking their toll on her stamina. Apparently, they hadn't affected the sheriff, however. He was pacing the room, his hands balled into fists.

"Where's Lucky? I assigned him to guard this room until Randy relieves him at midnight."

"Taking a dinner break, I imagine. You might try Lilly's Coffee Shop. But don't get all fired up at him. He hasn't had anyone to guard for hours. Besides, you're upsetting my patient. Her blood pressure is probably sky high after listening to you rant all day."

He grabbed Darlene's chart and started jotting down notes. "It's way past the dinner hour, but I can probably get one of the nurses to rummage up some food," he offered. "You don't need to miss any meals."

"No food for me," Darlene assured him, sitting on the

side of the bed and slipping off her shoes. "We stopped at Rosita's."

The doctor turned to Clint and frowned. "You wouldn't be letting your personal feelings interfere with your judgment, would you, Sheriff?"

Clint rapidly fisted and unfisted his hands. "Nothing personal about feeding a witness. Or about seeing that she isn't killed before she has a chance to talk. Reason enough to expect the guard on duty to actually be on duty."

The seriousness of Clint's tone didn't appear to affect the doctor. He just kept on about his business, nudging Clint out of the way and stepping to the head of Darlene's bed. "I take that to mean you haven't caught the men who attacked Darlene and McCord."

Clint fingered the brim of his hat. "No arrests yet. But we'll catch them."

"I'll be glad when you do. This just doesn't sound like McCord. He never slips up. Wouldn't have gotten where he is now if he did."

"McCord makes mistakes like everyone else," Clint said, walking over and checking the lock on the window. "He's human, in spite of his reputation."

"I still don't understand how he managed to be in a position where he could get attacked like that. Where was that security guard who tails him like a hound after a possum?"

"Bernie was off duty."

"See what I mean? Doesn't sound like Jim McCord. If he thought there was a chance of trouble, he'd have had Bernie on duty." Dr. Bennigan wrapped his fingers around Darlene's wrist to check her pulse. "How about you, Darlene? How's that head feel?"

"I've had a slight headache off and on, but very little dizziness."

"What about the memory?"

"I've remembered a few things. Nothing like what I'd hoped for."

The doctor's eyes grew kinder. "Maybe it's better for the time being. It'll give you a chance to rest and recover before dealing with the gruesome details of the attack. You know, sometimes our bodies shut down because they're a lot smarter than we are."

But the "gruesome details" were what she needed to remember. "I don't want any drugs of any kind tonight, Doctor. Write that on my chart. Absolutely no drugs, no matter what I might mutter in my sleep."

"I'll write it in red." He gave her a playful wink and turned back to Clint. "I can send a nurse in to stay with Darlene until your guard returns from his break. I need a few routine checks anyway. Temperature and blood pressure for the charts." He patted her on the top of the head the way he might a small child or a puppy.

"Afraid your nurse won't cut it," Clint answered, "unless she carries a revolver in her skirt pocket."

The doctor chuckled, and his glasses slid back down to the end of his nose. "The only weapon she has is a set of vocal cords you can hear all over the hospital."

He replaced the bed chart in its holder and stared at Clint, a frown tugging at his mouth. "You don't really think this man would just walk into the hospital and come after Darlene? I mean, he wouldn't be that crazy. Someone would surely see him."

"You're probably right. All the same, I'll wait around until Lucky returns."

The doctor nodded. "Makes sense. But I'll have to ask you to do your waiting outside. As soon as I give Darlene a thorough check, the nurse will help her get back into her hospital gown. She needs a good night's sleep.''

Once again they were talking around her, but this time Darlene didn't have the energy to complain. One sentence stuck in her mind. *You wouldn't be letting your personal feelings interfere with your judgment, would you, Sheriff?* A brief fling. That was how Clint had described their relationship. So why would the doctor think Clint's personal feelings would color his judgment six years later?

She stared at Clint, trying to imagine what it would have been like having him for a lover. To have those strong arms wrap around her, those lips crush hers. He would be gentle, but strong and exciting. The images intensified, and her pulse quickened. Thank goodness the doctor wasn't still holding her wrist.

The jarring ring of the telephone by her bed interrupted her torrid thoughts. She reached for the receiver. ''Hello.''

''Darlene, is that you?'' The urgency in the rough male voice sent alarms clanging through her head.

''Yes. Who is this?''

''Senator McCord. Are you alone?''

Darlene's lungs tightened, and she gasped for air. ''No, I'm not alone, Senator McCord, but I can talk.''

Clint crossed the room in an instant and moved to stand over her, motioning to her to keep McCord on the line.

''Everyone's worried about you,'' she said, struggling to find the right things to say, the right questions to ask.

''There's no reason to worry about me. I can take care of myself. But I need you to listen carefully. I can only talk a minute, Darlene.''

''Where are you?''

"I'm out of town, doing some research. It's better I don't say where, right now." He coughed to clear his throat. "I'm sorry for what happened Monday night. I didn't expect the attack," he continued. "I would never have called you if I thought there was a chance I was putting you in danger. I hope you know that."

Clint stuck a hastily scribbled note in her face. Darlene read the words into the phone. "Do you know who attacked us?"

"I'm working on that. Just listen for a minute, Darlene. This is very important, and I can't stay on the line much longer."

She pushed Clint's notes aside. "I'm listening. What is it you want me to do?"

"Have you told anyone what I told you the other night?"

"About what?" She was clutching at straws.

"The truth about my past."

"No, I've told no one."

"Good. Don't repeat any of it to anyone—not even the sheriff. I'll handle this my way. You did the right thing when you claimed to have amnesia. You were always a fast thinker."

"Anything else?"

"Yes. Talk to Clint Richards. Tell him I don't want him or any other cops on my tail. And I definitely don't want the FBI interfering with what I have to do. You make sure that they don't. I'm counting on you."

"Clint Richards is here now. You need to talk to him. He could help you." She was pleading now, sure that McCord was in trouble. "Just tell us who's after you."

"No. I wouldn't even if I could. You know too much already. Look, I have to go now. Just tell the sheriff I expect him to keep you safe. That's the real reason I called, Darlene. You're in danger, real danger. This man isn't sane. Do you understand?"

"No. I can't understand unless you tell me everything." Panic infiltrated her voice.

Clint yanked the receiver from her hand. "What's going on, McCord? And don't give me any runaround. I want it straight."

Darlene couldn't hear McCord's reply, but she saw fury grip Clint, twisting his face into hard lines.

Seconds later he slammed the receiver into the cradle.

CLINT WAS STILL fit to be tied when he brought his truck to a screeching stop in front of his front door. McCord had hung up on him, banged the receiver in his ear. Clint had gotten the message. McCord wanted no part of his help. No part of him. He never had.

It didn't matter. He'd lived his life without McCord's approval or his cooperation. And he definitely didn't need McCord telling him to protect Darlene from the lunatic *he'd* dragged into her life. He'd make damn sure Darlene was safe.

Darlene Remington, back in his life. If you'd asked him three days ago, he'd have sworn it was the last thing he wanted. The past was well behind him, his heart and mind finally clear of her, clear of the ache she'd left behind. Now it was starting all over again.

If he was near her, he wanted to touch her. If he touched her, he wanted to hold her close. If he held her, he wanted to make love to her.

This, after all the nights he'd vowed he'd never give her or any woman like her a chance to crawl under his skin, steal into his heart. Torment his very soul.

Then she'd dropped into his life again, hurt and afraid, and his promises had crashed as fast as a tin can in target practice. What had he ever done to deserve falling for the same woman twice? A woman who'd walk away again when this was over, the same way she had the first time.

Tired and distracted, he walked from the truck to the front door and stepped inside. Loopy jumped up, licking him everywhere his tongue would reach. Clint rewarded the mutt with an absentminded pat. Loopy didn't settle for that. He jumped up again, this time barking incessantly.

"Calm down, boy. I've got a couple of calls to make before I can play." One was to a newsman out of Austin who'd somehow gotten wind of the fact that McCord and a pretty FBI agent had gotten attacked while they were parked in a secluded area. Alone. At night. Said he'd heard the woman's husband had trailed them and tried to kill them both.

A little truth. A little rumor. Now Clint would have to convince him the story was all rumor. Clint would still trade a market-ready steer himself to know exactly what Darlene and McCord were doing parked ten miles past nowhere in the dark on Monday evening, but he was convinced now that the meeting had nothing to do with a physical relationship. Darlene was too smart for that. Besides, Mary had made it clear that Darlene had come to town at McCord's urging, and that she hadn't a clue as to what he wanted.

Clint dropped to the couch and used the heel of his right boot to pry off the left. He reached over and scratched Loopy behind the ear with one hand as he reached for the phone with the other. How was he going to convince a newsman not to print a juicy sex scandal about a leading political figure, a story fueled by facts and littered with lies.

"Thank you, Senator McCord," he muttered wryly.
Loopy barked his opinion.

DARLENE SHOOK AWAKE, her fingers brushing the edge
of the bandage and then rubbing the dregs of sleep from
her eyes. She rolled over and looked at the clock. Ten
minutes past two. Something must have wakened her.

She listened, but even the routine sounds of the hospital were absent. Nothing much going on, the night
nurse had said. One new baby in the nursery, an appen-
dectomy in the children's wing, and a few elderly patients
battling flu or pneumonia. The nurses were probably in
the snack room, chatting and having a cup of coffee before the early morning activities jumped into full swing.

Uneasy quivers attacked her stomach. Paranoia. She
had to fight it. The guard was right outside her door.

Reaching across the pillow, she ran her fingers along
the edge of the mattress, searching for the control that
turned on the reading lamp. One of the nurses had left a
copy of *Southern Living* on her nightstand. Since she
couldn't sleep, she might as well give it a look.

The control was missing. Someone must have moved
it to keep her from calling for help. The nurse from last
night, the one who'd given her the shot when she knew
Darlene didn't want to be drugged?

No, she was only imagining things. She forced her
heartbeat to slow. Paranoia was common among amnesia
patients. She wouldn't give in to it.

She took deep breaths, but the fear grew worse. Someone was in this room, in the dark, watching her. She
could feel him. Her breath caught. This wasn't another
dream. She was awake.

"Randy. Randy!"

Her door squeaked open. The beam of his flashlight

darted about the room, but it was long, unbearable seconds before his reassuring voice eased her terror. "I'm right here, Darlene. Is something wrong?"

"I can't find my control for the lights. It must have fallen."

"I'll get it for you. Mind if I turn on the overhead light?"

"No, I don't mind." In fact, nothing would please her more. Her pounding heart eased to near normal as bright light flooded the room. Randy stood by the door, his hand resting on the butt of the gun he wore at his waist.

She let her gaze trail every inch of space. The curtain that circled her bed when privacy was needed was bunched against the wall, unmoving. The bouquet of flowers on the windowsill no longer cast strange, elongated shadows on the wall.

Paranoia. Alive and well and residing in the FBI-agent-turned-coward.

Randy sauntered toward the bed. "You look mighty pale. Want me to go get one of the nurses?"

"No, I must have had another bad dream. I'm fine. Do you see the control?"

He stooped and looked under the edge of the bed. Darlene spied it then, on the bedside table.

"I found it," she said, reaching around the bed rail to retrieve it. "The nurse must have unclipped it when she straightened my sheets. I'm sorry I bothered you."

"No bother. Truth is, I was getting pretty lonely out there. Want me to sit with you a spell?"

She hated to hurt his feelings, but she really didn't. Now that her fears had been alleviated, she would be happier alone, thinking, trying to make sense of everything that had happened the last few days—especially tonight's phone call from McCord.

"I appreciate the offer, but I'd better get some sleep. If all goes well, I plan to check out of the hospital tomorrow."

"Really? I hadn't heard that."

"Neither have I, but I plan to pursue it. The headaches have all but stopped."

"Are you going back to Washington?"

"Not for a few days. I'll stay at the motel in town. Or maybe at the Altamira. Apparently I was already on their guest list."

"I'll have to get better acquainted with that cute redheaded nurse tonight then."

She smiled and watched Randy back out the door, flashing her an easy smile that showed a sparkling set of crooked white teeth just before he clicked off the light.

She settled back into the bed. The nagging pain started again just above her right temple, but it was nothing she couldn't live with. A little pain was far better than narcotics that dulled her senses and compounded the confusion of the amnesia.

The heat cranked on. She snuggled beneath the covers, lulled by the hum of the motor and the warmth. And the fact that Randy was right outside her door.

Something clattered, but she refused to give in to paranoia again. It was only the night sounds of an old building and noisy equipment. She closed her eyes tightly, determined to will the fear away.

Only it didn't go away. It grew worse. Someone was near. She could hear their breathing, hear their footsteps on the tile floor. Her eyes flew open.

She struggled to scream as a hand shot from the darkness and strangled her cries.

"It's too late, FBI babe. The game is over."

The man's lips were at her ear, one hand shoving her

face into the bed, the other shoving something into her mouth. This couldn't be happening. She was being murdered in a hospital bed with an armed guard steps away.

She coughed, trying to dislodge the wad of foul-tasting cloth. It was stifling her breath, killing her screams. Summoning every ounce of strength she could find, she threw her body upward, felt her body rise and then slam back against the mattress.

"You're a strong little bitch. Just not strong enough."

She lunged forward and her head crashed against what felt like his head. He mumbled a curse, and his grip on her arm grew slack. Fighting hard, she yanked her hand sideways in the split second before he gained full control.

But the man was too quick for her. He held her down, his fingers digging into her neck and squeezing, like a rope in a hanging knot. She felt her body folding, giving in to the lack of oxygen, giving up. With one heaving movement, she jerked as hard as she could, throwing her hips against the metal rod that was supposed to keep her from falling out of the high bed.

The metal rattled, mingling with her attacker's low curses. She gasped one last time as the blackness pulled her under.

Her last thoughts were of Clint, wishing he were here.

Chapter Six

Clint swerved into the first available parking spot in front of the hospital. It was the middle of the night, way too late for making visits, but he had an urge to check on Darlene.

Probably born of the phone call that had wakened him in the middle of the night. *Keep your nose out of the senator's problems or you'll die with him and his FBI girlfriend.*

He'd nearly exploded with fury when he'd hung up the phone. The senator had stirred up a mess of real trouble this time, and it was boiling over into a lot more lives than his. If this was what it meant to be the man of the people, Clint was thankful he was just a lowly member of the unknown masses.

Still running on an adrenaline overload, he pushed through the glass door of the hospital. He turned the corner and spied Randy, all smiles and chatting with a red-headed nurse. Irritation rattled his control. Randy was yards away from Darlene's room, but at least he was facing in the right direction.

The deputy turned as Clint headed toward him. "You're up and about late, Sheriff."

"I've had a busy night." He nodded toward Darlene's

room and the chair Randy had vacated right outside her door. "Looks like you've wandered a ways from your post." His tone was harsher than it needed to be, but so were attacks and threats of murder.

"Just stretching my legs for a second. I haven't been standing here two minutes, and I haven't been out of sight of that door. I'm doing my job, if that's what's got you riled, Clint. I told you earlier—you can count on me to keep Darlene safe."

"I'll vouch for him." The nurse flashed Clint a warm smile.

"I'm not looking for a voucher. I just expect my witness to be guarded every second of the night."

"She's fine, Clint," Randy said, watching the backside of the nurse as she walked away. "Darlene, I mean. I was just in her room."

"Is she awake?"

"She was a few minutes ago. She'd lost the controls to the light over her bed, and I went in to help her find it. Offered to stay and chat a spell, but she said she wasn't in the mood for company. Are you going in to see her this time of the night?"

"I'm going to stick my head in." He started to walk away but thought better of it. Randy was young, but he showed promise as a lawman. He just needed to learn that when Clint gave an order, he meant for it to be followed. "In the future, I expect you to either be in Darlene's room or right outside it."

"I could hear a scream from here."

"I want you near enough to hear a footstep or a whisper." Clint stepped closer, lowering his voice even more. "I had a phone call a little earlier, telling me that Darlene was as good as dead."

Randy rammed his hands in the back pockets of his

jeans and rocked back on his heels. "Lowlifes. Damn lowlifes got no business breathing good folks' air."

Clint moved into Randy's space. "This man is as dangerous as they come. When you're on duty, I expect you to guard Darlene like it was your own mother you were watching over. Do you follow me?"

"I hear you loud and clear, Sheriff. I'll glue myself to her door."

Clint started toward her room. He wouldn't wake her if she was asleep. He just wanted to sit by her for a while. Maybe it was hearing that voice on the phone tonight. Maybe it was his growing awareness that Monday night could have turned out a whole lot worse. All he was sure of was that he ached to be near her, to hold her hand in his, to make sure she was all right.

He'd spent years trying to forget what it had been like to have her in his life, what it had been like to love her. The years had been wasted. The feelings were still inside him, as strong as ever.

His fingers wrapped around the doorknob. It turned, but the door didn't move. Surely she didn't have it locked! He tried it again, panic and adrenaline shooting through him.

"Darlene, are you in there?"

A low moan from inside. He reared back and kicked as hard as he could. On the second try, the door flew open and he rushed in.

Yanking the pistol from his holster with his right hand, he fumbled for the light switch with the other. The light flashed on, and he reeled at what he saw. In less than a second, he was holding Darlene in his arms, yanking the gag from her mouth.

The next he was off and running, screaming for Randy

to get the nurse while he jumped through an open window on the trail of a would-be killer.

"FIND ME SOME CLOTHES. I want out of here. Now."

Clint lay on his most intimidating glare while trying to come up with an argument that would convince Darlene she was in the best place for her. "You're too weak to walk."

"Then get me a wheelchair."

"Be reasonable, Darlene. You had a close call last night. You're nauseated, confused and—"

"Alive. Barely. Which I wouldn't be if you hadn't arrived last night the second you did."

A fact he didn't need to be reminded of. The way he felt when he'd burst into her room would haunt him forever.

In a romantic movie, he'd be at her bedside now, holding her in his arms, telling her that. But Darlene had her own ideas about the role she was supposed to play. Instead of clinging to him in gratitude, she was giving him orders.

"Dr. Bennigan will never release you today, Darlene, not after what you went through last night. Besides, you know what I told you. It's here or jail. I can't just let you walk the streets on your own."

"Why not? I'd be safer on the streets than I was here with an armed guard."

He threw up his hands in exasperation. "We've been through that."

"I know, and I'm not blaming you or Randy. And I'm sure Dr. Bennigan is a very good doctor. But somebody is trying to kill me. McCord warned us the man was crazy enough to try anything."

"Yeah. Too bad McCord didn't also tell us who the man is."

Darlene swung her bare legs over the side of the bed. "He can't. I've thought about it, and the only reasonable answer is that McCord doesn't know who's behind the trouble."

"So where is McCord? He could have told you that."

"So that you could hire an armed guard to protect him?"

Clint ticked the wall with his index finger. "Score one for you, for whatever it's worth. But that doesn't get us any closer to catching up with McCord or finding out what he's involved in."

He had to quit thinking of Darlene as a defenseless victim—regardless of the fact that she couldn't remember her past. Every day she settled deeper into the persona of Darlene Remington, FBI agent. And, according to reputation, she was one of the best.

"I think McCord's on the run, hiding somewhere and hoping the men who are after him will be captured," she continued.

"McCord? You've got the wrong man. He doesn't hide from trouble. He thrives on it. Besides, if he were waiting for someone to catch these guys, he wouldn't have called off the FBI and told me to stay out of it."

Darlene slid off the bed, holding onto the rail for support. New bruises colored her arms and darkened her cheeks. The sight ground in Clint's gut. She'd been in his protective custody. He'd let her down. And no matter how insistent she became, it wouldn't happen again.

Clint stopped pacing and stared out the window. It was better when he didn't look at Darlene, when he couldn't look into her eyes, couldn't see the shimmering fire that awakened old urges. "You need to forget McCord and concentrate on only one thing, Darlene. Get your memory back. Leave the rest to me.''

Darlene joined him at the window. ''Then tell me more about McCord, Clint. You say you aren't friends, but you must like him. I mean you talk about him like he's tough and brave. A cop's kind of guy.''

''He is tough and brave. And too smart not to have an idea what's going on and who's behind it. And I resent like hell that he dragged you into the middle of his mess.''

''We were friends. He wanted my help. Now I can't even remember what he told me.'' Her voice wavered. ''My memory loss—it always comes back to that.'' She turned and leaned against the wall.

Clint softened in spite of himself. She blamed so much of this on her amnesia. No wonder she was so determined to do something to help.

''You've had a tough few days,'' he said, determined to talk some sense into her. ''The best way to regain your memory is to get some rest and quit trying to solve a mystery you're ill-equipped to handle.''

''And I won't get a good night's rest in this hospital.'' Darlene tugged on his arm, made him face her. ''I won't stay here another night, Clint. I can't. Not with the man who wants me dead still on the loose.''

''No one will hurt you tonight. I'm taking the duty myself. If he shows up again, I'll be ready for him.''

''I have a better idea. Go get me the clothes I wore yesterday. I don't know why you had the nurse take them out of my room to start with.''

''To keep you from sneaking out.''

''Sneaking past an armed guard. That's overkill, don't you think? Anyway, I won't sneak out. I'll leave with you and stay at your place tonight.''

At his place. Just the two of them. If that happened, she'd need protection from more than the killer. "I don't run a guest house," he said. "I have one bed, and it's not too comfortable."

"I don't care about comfort. If you won't let me leave on my own, then take me with you, Clint."

Her words squeezed around his heart, but she was asking too much. How would he ever let her go again if he saw her in the morning, all tousled and sleepy-eyed? If he saw her skin glistening from the shower, or caught a glimpse of her nestled in his bed?

"Please, Clint. Take me home with you. We can talk. You can tell me about McCord, give me something to help me recall what he said to me Monday night."

"You don't give up, do you?"

"Not when it's this important. I can't."

No, the only thing she'd ever given up on had been the two of them. And he'd damn well better keep that in mind.

"You win," he said, regretting the words the second they left his lips.

"You won't be sorry. Who knows? I might even be able to cook."

She stepped toward him, her bandaged head cocked to one side, and his heart plunged. If her body was as strong as her will, he might be able to keep his cool, hide the feelings that snaked through him. But she was frail, shaky.

She weaved slightly, and he caught her in his arms. She clung to him, and desire shot through him, so intense that his whole body grew hard. He forced himself to loosen his grip, but she didn't move away.

"Sorry, cowboy. I guess I lost my balance there."

Her words were flippant. Her tone wasn't. The words came out in a shaky purr.

"No problem." Clint tipped his hat and backed away, knowing he was lying. There were a couple of problems, both of them Texas-size: a psychotic killer loose in his town, and Darlene Remington sleeping in his bed.

It didn't get much worse than this.

NOTHING HAD CHANGED, the situation was no less serious, yet Darlene felt far more confident that everything would turn out right now that she was out of the hospital for good.

Even the turban-like bandage had been swapped for a smaller one. Sitting up straight, she pulled down the visor for a look in the mirror. Less than attractive, but it could be much worse. She could be dead.

Clint glanced in her direction. "You're still the prettiest lady around these parts."

"Thanks," she murmured. The compliment took her totally by surprise. She didn't know the rough, tough sheriff had it in him to pay compliments. But then, he hadn't seemed either rough or tough this afternoon when he'd held her to keep her from falling.

She turned back to the window as a crazy, giddy feeling skidded through her. She and Clint had been lovers. Her mind couldn't recall the details, but apparently her body hadn't forgotten.

Clint settled back into silence, and she returned to the task of searching for familiar landmarks out the window. They passed miles of pasture inside barbwire fences with little to break the monotony. Then she braced herself as Clint swerved left onto a dirt road. "Is your ranch near the Altamira?"

"Nope. Mine's west of town. And don't expect it to

compare with the Altamira. My folks liked the simple life, and it was just fine by me. Still is.''

"You still live with your folks? I never took you for a mama's boy.'' She was teasing, and surprised at how good it felt.

"I took over my parents' original bungalow when they built a bigger place. My parents are both dead now.''

So much for teasing. Leave it to her to open mouth and insert foot. "I'm sorry.''

Clint kept his eyes on the road. "It's okay. It was a long time ago.''

She turned back to the window. "Are you sure we're not on the road to the Altamira? I'd swear I saw that red lopsided barn last night.''

"I didn't say we weren't going out to McCord's place. I just said I didn't live by him.''

"I should learn to ask the right questions.''

"I'd say asking questions is definitely your strong suit.'' Clint offered one of his rare smiles, a broad one that lit up his face, and Darlene's stomach did a somersault. The man was much too attractive to have stayed single so long.

"So why are we going to McCord's ranch?'' she asked, deciding questions were more productive than her current thoughts.

"To get your things, and to talk to Freddie Caulder. He called right before we left the hospital, all upset about something. Said he needed to talk to me right away. I figured you could visit with Mary while he and I meet.''

"What kind of things do I have at McCord's?''

"Your luggage. That's where I got the clothes you're wearing now. You didn't think I'd bought them, did you?''

Luggage. Why hadn't she thought of that? It wasn't

that he'd guessed what size jeans she wore. Or that he'd gone to the store and picked out lacy flesh-colored panties. He'd just dug through her own things and decided what she needed.

"Why didn't you just bring all my clothes to the hospital?"

"You would have had to rent space. You either planned to stay in town a while, or you expected to change clothes a lot. My guess is you were planning to hang around a while, do a little moonlighting for McCord. He must have needed information he thought you could get for him. Unofficially, of course."

There it was again. That resentment that tainted his voice every time he talked about the senator. "Tell me about McCord. I know he's on the fast track to the White House. The morning paper said he's leading the current list of contenders by twenty percent. And he hasn't even officially announced his candidacy, though the reporter seemed to think McCord had definitely made up his mind to run."

"And run he did—right out of town. What do you want to know about him?" he asked, pushing on the accelerator.

"For starters, what's his family like? Does he get along with them?"

"He has one daughter, Levi."

"The one who was in the photograph we were looking at the other night."

"Right. He adores her, lavishes her with attention and gifts. And he has a niece named Robin who helps Whitt Emory manage McCord's campaign."

"Is McCord divorced?"

"No. His wife died when Levi was just a kid. He

raised her himself, with the help of Mary. The perfect father figure.''

"What about his past? Is there anything that would make him a target, make someone come after him to kill him?''

Clint drummed his fingers on the steering wheel. "I don't know that you need anything these days. All the loonies in the country are stirred up over the upcoming millennium. The ones who aren't shouting that the world is coming to an end on its own are threatening to end it themselves. All the attention McCord's getting in the press is bound to make him a target.''

"Then no wonder he called me.'' Darlene faced Clint, sliding her left leg onto the seat between them. "The FBI would be the logical ones to check that out.''

"The FBI—not you personally.'' His muscles tensed, his arms straining against the fabric of his shirt. "This is something personal—a score someone plans to settle with McCord. What gets me is that he got you involved and then ran off without giving us a clue as to who's trying to kill you.''

Clint muttered the words through clenched teeth, and Darlene lay a calming hand on his leg. She shouldn't have. He jumped at her touch as if she'd been holding a lit match.

Maybe she'd made a mistake, insisting he take her home with him. Every touch, every look between them ignited something. Burning embers that still held fire?

"If I've done something that upset you, Clint, either now or in the past, you can tell me. Maybe if we bring it out in the open, we can get past it.''

Clint's hands gripped the steering wheel, his back straight, his gaze focused on the road in front of him. "I got past everything that was between us years ago.''

"But maybe I didn't."

They rode the rest of the way to the Altamira in silence.

DARLENE SIPPED the second cup of tea Mary had poured, the restlessness inside her growing with every minute Clint and Freddie stayed away.

"Why don't you and Clint stay for supper?" Mary urged. "I've got a big pot of soup and a pan of corn bread. Half of it will go to waste if you don't."

"I'll have to ask Clint. I don't know what plans he has for the evening." Darlene twirled her cup, watching the dark liquid circle the rim. "He and Freddie have been gone a long time. I think I might walk outside and try to find them."

"I wouldn't. But you were never one to sit back and let the men do all the talking and worrying. That's probably why Jim was so tickled when you decided to join up with the FBI."

"Did I visit here often when I was younger?"

"You did when you were in high school. You were older than Levi, but the two of you hit it off from the start. Probably because you both love horses and riding so much. But mostly, you liked talking to the senator, following him around like a starstruck teenager. We guessed it was because your own parents were dead, and all you had was your granny."

Mary walked over to the stove and stirred the soup. "Of course, once you took up with Clint, all that changed. The two of you were thicker than molasses that summer before you went to Quantico. We were all geared up for a wedding, but I guess the lure of the FBI got into your blood and pushed romance out of your heart."

"Then you don't really know why Clint and I broke up."

"No, but I know it was none of the sheriff's doing. That boy moped around for months after you left. Still is moping, for all I know. He hasn't taken up with any of the local ladies, and it's not because they haven't tried."

"Very interesting." Darlene put down her cup and grabbed her jacket from the hook by the door. "I think I'll walk down to the barn and check on Clint and Freddie. They've had the pleasure of avoiding our company far too long."

Darlene headed toward the barn, her feet rustling the dry grass. The sun had disappeared completely, but the moon was out and the sky sparkled with stars so close that she could have sworn she could touch them.

The cool night air wrapped around her, and a chilly tremble sneaked into her heart. *Danger.* She wasn't supposed to feel that here—not with the ranch security system McCord had in place.

She stopped and forced her lungs to suck in a healthy gulp of air. Still, she could feel darkness and fear closing in all around her—

Memories tore through her mind. She could see the man, could see the gun. She covered her ears as he pulled the trigger. But the man fell to the ground.

The memories were as vivid as if she were watching a video in slow motion. Terrifying memories.

Only they weren't hers.

Chapter Seven

"I'm just telling you how I heard it, Clint. McCord don't want you sticking your nose into his business. So, butt out."

"I'm the law around here. That's not an option."

Freddie rubbed at a day's growth of stubble on his weathered chin. "McCord don't need your help. He said it, and now I'm saying it. And neither of us have anything personal against you."

"Right, nothing personal between me and McCord." Clint propped a foot on the bale of alfalfa hay where Freddie sat, but his eyes circled the old storage shed where McCord's foreman had brought him to talk.

Out of the wind and the night air and away from the womenfolk. That's what he'd said when he dragged Clint out of the house to the shed. First, he'd hemmed and hawed and talked about everything from feed prices to the local high-school football team, but Freddie had finally gotten down to the nitty-gritty: McCord knew Clint was continuing the investigation after he'd told him to stop, and he was not pleased.

"Stay out of it, Clint. Forget the attack. McCord will handle it."

"And what about the attempt on Darlene's life last

night? Would McCord have me just sweep that under the rug too? Is he going to be responsible when the lunatic comes calling again?''

"He'd sent word for you to protect her. You didn't. Now he wants Darlene out of town. He'll hire protection for her. Men that can be relied on to do what they're told to do. He wants you to have Darlene on a plane back to D.C. in the morning.''

"And if I don't dance to McCord's fiddle?''

"Then it might not be too healthy for you around here.''

Clint bent to the rotting wooden floor and picked up a rusted hay rake. He stood it upright and leaned on it, looking at Freddie face on so there would be no mistaking his meaning.

"You tell McCord that if he has something to say to me, he needs to call me *personally*. He can start by apologizing for hanging up on me yesterday. After that, he can say his piece, but I'm not kowtowing to him like everyone else does. I'm the law in this county, and I'm not backing off from my duty.''

Clint leaned in closer, purposely intimidating the foreman. "And if my investigations lead me to finding McCord and sticking my nose into his business, so be it.''

Clint expected Freddie to bristle, but, if anything, the man looked relieved. The unexpected reaction took Clint by surprise. He'd have to think on it some more later. Right now, he needed to get back to Darlene and take her home.

Home. To his bed. He shrugged off the disturbing urges that sneaked into his mind and body. He tossed the rake aside, ready to get on his way. A moan wafted through the partially open door.

"Sounds like Mary's cat has her tail caught in a crack again," Freddie said, reaching down to pick up the rake and move it out of his path.

The sound grew closer. A cat, or a woman crying for help. Clint raced to the door, his brain fighting images his heart couldn't bear to see. If something had happened to Darlene…

One step into the night air, and his heart sank. Darlene was stumbling toward him, her head down, sobs shaking her body. Swiftly crossing the ground between them, he swept her into his arms. She melted against him, clinging as if she'd never let him go.

"What's wrong?" he whispered. "What happened?"

She shook her head and clung all the tighter, her body pressing hard against his own. He held her until she quieted, his hands stroking her back, his chin nestled on top of her head. Poor baby, she'd been through so much and had remained so strong until now. But she was only human.

And the doctor had warned him. She was likely to have sinking spells: times when the amnesia became too frightful and frustrating for her to handle alone.

"Is there something I can say or do?" He felt the inadequacy of manhood more strongly than he ever had before. Give him a criminal to apprehend, cattle to round up, a bull to manhandle. But don't give him a tearful woman. All he knew to do was hold her.

Long seconds later, she pulled away from him and breathed raggedly. "It was so real," she murmured. "I was there, standing with the soldiers. So close I felt the sting of the bullet, the heat of the fire."

He dug in his back pocket for his handkerchief, and blotted overflowing tears from her eyes. "What was real, Darlene? What are you talking about?"

She shook her head, and wispy strands of cinnamon-colored hair fell into her face. He stroked them away. The coolness of her cheek on his hand added to his uneasiness. "What's real? Tell me."

"Memories." Her voice broke, and she trembled but pushed away gently and stood on her own now, staring into space. "I was standing in the open with a group of men. They were in army fatigues, dirty, unshaven. One second they were talking. The next they were screaming at each other—loud, angry curses."

Blind fury raced rampant through Clint. Was this what had happened Monday night, what McCord had hauled her into? No wonder she had crushed the memories.

"It's okay, Darlene." He wrapped his arms around her again, but this time she was rigid, unreachable. Scared senseless, he was sure. "You're safe now," he whispered, burying his fingers through the hair that curled at the nape of her neck. "Tell me everything you remember, and I'll make sure this is over."

"No, you don't understand." She turned back to the path she'd followed to find him. "*I* don't understand. All I know is these weren't *my* memories."

"Hold on, sweetheart." He rocked her to him, aching to suck her pain inside himself and steal it away from her. He tilted her head up and grew sick at the terror mirrored in her eyes.

"It's not you, Darlene. It's the amnesia. But you'll be all right. The hard part is behind you."

"No, Clint. It's not behind me." She pulled away. "Nothing is settled." She closed her eyes, and tears spilled onto her cheeks.

He led her into the shed and tugged her to a bale of hay, all the while cradling her beneath his arm. He'd never seen her like this. Even last night when she'd looked death in the eye, she hadn't been this devastated. Still, this signaled a breakthrough. Apparently she'd remembered something of what had transpired on Monday night. It was just all jumbled with fears created in her own mind.

"How much of your past do you remember, Darlene?"

"None. At least I don't think so. Have I ever been in combat?"

"You weren't in the service. Maybe you were in some sort of training program that resembled combat."

"This wasn't a mock situation. It was real. Too real." Her voice quaked, but the tears had stopped. And her face had regained a smidgen of color.

"I think we should get you back to the hospital—let Dr. Bennigan check you over."

"No, I can't go back. I have to go forward, face this down and find out what's happening to my mind."

He stroked her back, ran his thumb up and down the curve of her neck. That's when he realized Freddie was still standing in the shadows, watching.

"Why don't you go on in and check on Mary, Freddie? I'll take care of Darlene."

Clint watched him back away. He'd been nervous the whole time he and Clint had talked. Now he looked as if he was walking in a trance. Clint hated to think about what kind of stories would be spread about Darlene. And in a town this size, gossip traveled faster than a farmer to supper.

"I was there, Clint, and yet I wasn't." She sought out his gaze. "Do you think I'm going crazy?"

"No. I don't know what to make of this, but not that." He buried his lips in her silky hair, needing the closeness now as much as she did. "Let's don't talk about it now.

It will make more sense later, when you've had time to gain some perspective."

"Will that ever happen?"

"When this is over. When the man who tried to kill you is caught and your true memory returns, you'll put these nightmares behind you."

"I only wish they were nightmares. That I could open my eyes and they would disappear."

And so did Clint. He helped her to her feet. She was frail, defenseless, the way she'd been the night he'd found her on Glenn Road. It wouldn't last, though. She was too strong. A night's rest, and she'd transform back to the woman she'd always been: brave, feisty, ready to take on the world. She might doubt it, but he didn't, not for a minute.

He led her toward the house.

"Not back to the hospital, Clint. I won't go back there."

"I know." He put his lips on hers. "I'm taking you home."

"Oh, m'gosh!" Darlene exclaimed as she entered the kitchen in Clint's house. "It's ten-thirty in the morning. Why didn't you wake me before now?"

"I don't know if I could have. Not only have I clattered around in here all morning, but Loopy took up a barking frenzy when he heard Randy's truck drive up about an hour ago. You slept right through it." Clint smiled.

She rubbed her eyes and headed straight for the coffeepot. Lifting it off the range, she shook it gently. "Is this stuff still decent?"

"All depends on what you call 'decent.' I made it a few minutes ago, so it's fresh."

She picked up the pottery mug he'd left out for her and filled her cup. Propping her backside against his Formica counter, she sipped the brew and then made a face. "You do know you're supposed to add water to the grounds, don't you?"

"I like it strong." He sat back and watched her, relief sweetening a morning that had gotten off to a bad start. Even after they'd arrived back at his place last night and talked about the images she'd experienced, she'd been quiet, visibly shaken.

Now, this morning she was her old self, sassy as ever. Too much her old self. If he half tried, he could almost believe they had drifted back in time, picked up where they'd left off, with mornings full of teasing and laughter. Full of passion.

"My granddad always said coffee should be bitter and women sweet," he said, determined not to let his memories do him in.

"And you followed his advice, I see."

"I try. I usually succeed with the coffee part of the formula."

"Perhaps you have different tastes in women than your granddad. Sweet is not all it's cracked up to be, except in too-strong coffee and peanut-butter fudge."

"Sleep apparently did you good," he said, pushing back the stack of faxed responses Randy had delivered earlier.

She carried her coffee to the table and took the kitchen chair opposite his. "About last night..."

He waved her off. "Why don't we delve into that subject after you've had breakfast? I can fry up some bacon and scramble you some eggs straight from Betsy Crow's henhouse."

"Eggs straight from the hen. I bet I never had that in D.C."

"See what you've been missing?"

She toyed with the fringed edge of a dishcloth that peeked from under a section of the morning newspaper. "I've noticed several things I've probably been missing. Eggs isn't one of them."

The timbre of her voice was noticeably seductive. Clint gripped the pen in his hand the way he needed to grip his resolve. Grabbing his empty cup, he pushed back from the table and walked over to refill it. Before Darlene had woken up and walked into his kitchen in her cute little bunny pajamas, he'd convinced himself that he could handle this situation.

Now he wasn't so sure. He'd have to keep their relationship as focused as possible on the unsolved mystery. If he let his emotions rule, he'd fall victim to his own needs.

"Have I been in this house before, Clint? Is this where you lived when we were…when we dated?" She scooted her chair around to face him.

He considered his answer, and damned her poor timing. "You spent some time here. Not a lot. We were only together one summer."

"The summer before I went to Quantico for my training." She scanned the room. "I feel comfortable here, not at all like the hospital. Almost like I belong. I didn't wake up once during the night." She walked over and ran her fingers along the hem of gingham curtain at the window. "I was just thinking—it might be my memory breaking free, responding to familiar surroundings."

"Could be. Those curtains were your addition," he said, ignoring the lump that had settled in his chest. "You said my place was too drab. 'Nothing but cowboy clutter.' I think that's how you put it.''

She winced. "I wasn't too tactful, was I?"

"You were honest."

"I hope that wasn't my best quality."

"Not nearly." He didn't elaborate. It wouldn't be in the interest of self-preservation.

Pulling back the curtains, she stared out at the biggest oak tree on his property. Past that was his corral. There was a chestnut at the fence, head held high as if he knew he had an admirer.

She finished her coffee and ambled back to her chair. The expression on her face had taken a turn to the serious. "About last night…"

"After breakfast. Dr. Bennigan said you needed to eat. Part of your recovery plan."

"Just toast then. I wouldn't want you to lose your nursing credentials."

Clint stripped the plastic closure from the bread and popped a couple of slices into the toaster. Toast, and then talk. He'd spent half the night going over the bizarre events she'd described last night and had come up with only one answer. A long shot. But if he was right, this would be the first real clue of the case.

First toast, then he'd nail her with his take on what she'd pictured in her mind last night. It wouldn't be a fair trade-off.

"JUST BREATHE THAT AIR." Darlene threw her head back and took another lung-filling gulp. "I feel as if I've been cooped up for weeks instead of days." She barely controlled the urge to skip ahead of Clint as they neared the corral.

"It beats hibernating inside four walls."

"Definitely. I think we should have our talk right over there." She pointed toward a sunny spot just east of the corral. "That way we have a view of the horses and the hillside."

"Looks like as good a spot as any."

"But first, I think we should stop and say hello to the chestnut who's prancing around the fence, explain to him why we can't take him for a ride."

"That's Brandy. And you aren't trying to put off the inevitable, are you?"

She gave his question some thought. "The last few days have been like a living hell. This morning, I feel like I've escaped the heat for a few hours, landed in a temporary haven where things have at least a vague sense of normalcy. I guess I am hesitant to jump back into the chaos and fear."

That said, she danced ahead of Clint and climbed to the first rung of the wooden fence. "Here, boy, come talk to me." The chestnut loped over to the fence and poked his head over the top rail.

Darlene rubbed Brandy's long neck, whispering to him all the while about what a beautiful and regal creature he was. The actions came as naturally to her as brushing her teeth or dressing herself. Meaning, she must have done this many times before. She turned to find Clint standing a few yards behind, not walking, only watching her.

He probably thought she was some kind of dingbat, crooning to a horse when he was waiting to talk to her about the next steps in finding a man bent on being her executioner. But here, at Clint's ranch, the terrifying events of the past few days seemed more surreal than ever.

Yet nothing had really changed except her setting. The images that had emerged last night hadn't lost their sub-

stance. Images so vivid she had felt the heat of the blaz-
ing fire that had raged through a deserted village, and the
terror of an event she could never have known in real
life.

The horse neighed and backed away from her, tapping
the ground with his right front hoof and tossing his head
to the side. His keen perception had picked up the switch
in her mood even before she had. Darlene had let the
images back into her mind, and the false veil of normalcy
had vanished as quickly as smoke in the wind.

"That's no way to treat your favorite lady, Brandy.
Not when it's been so long since she's come calling on
us."

Clint's lips at Darlene's ear reassured her and the cautious chestnut. Brandy eased back to the fence, and
pressed his cheek against Clint's outstretched hand.

"So Brandy's part of the past I don't remember."

"You talked me into buying him from McCord, and
then persuaded the senator to give me a sweetheart of a
deal."

She reached across Clint and scratched Brandy's forehead. "And then I moved away and left you. No wonder
you haven't forgiven me, Brandy."

"That would be asking a lot."

Clint's voice was husky, revealing, leaving no doubt
that he was no longer referring to Brandy. There was a
crazy, undefined fluttering across her nerve endings. She
had once made love to the rugged, devastatingly hand-
some sheriff that stood at her elbow. Had she walked
away, as his statement indicated? Left Vaquero, left this
ranch, left this man whose arms she ached to crawl into
this very minute?

If she had, she hoped she'd had a very good reason.

She climbed down from the fence. "I guess it's time we had our talk," she said.

"Yeah." Clint gave Brandy a parting love pat, and started toward the spot Darlene had chosen earlier, not bothering to wait for her. "The business at hand. That's the reason you're here."

She joined him, kicking away an assortment of twigs before she smoothed a seat in the carpet of dry leaves. "Looks like my idea to talk outside might have been a bad one, after all," she said, spying the clouds that had gathered and darkened over their heads.

"The rain should hold off long enough for us to finish our discussion."

Clint fingered the brim of his hat, a habit when he had a lot on his mind. Darlene was amazed at the things she'd learned about him in such a short time. Possibly because she had no past to muddy her recall. "So, what shall we talk about?" she said, knowing full well that Clint had plans for the conversation he'd said they needed to put off until after breakfast.

"Are you ready to talk about the images you experienced at the Altamira last night?"

"I would be if they made any sense."

"I have a theory about them." Clint hunched down beside her, drawing a series of short, straight lines in the earth with a sharp twig. "The theory's not tied together with a strong lariat, but it's a place to start."

"Not tied together because I lost the rope in the misty caverns of my mind."

"A matter of time. I see lots of signs your memory's returning."

"Fill me in." She stretched her legs in front of her, pushing brown oak leaves into a pile at the heel of her boots. "I could use some encouraging news."

"You think and frequently talk like someone in law enforcement. You moved around my house last night and this morning like someone who'd been there before, opening the right drawers, even getting extra towels."

"You never said anything about it," she said, realizing he was right.

"I didn't want to draw your attention to it. When you concentrate on remembering, you get overwhelmed with frustration. You do better if you just go with the flow, let the memories find their own way of surfacing."

"You are a very intuitive man, Sheriff Clint Richards. Only one of your talents, I expect."

He cocked his head sideways, and she caught a glimpse of his eyes and a glimmer of something that looked like...desire. She leaned against the trunk, imagining what other talents he might have, then deciding this was not the time to go there.

"Talents such as the ability to come up with the theory you're about to share with me," she added, attempting to get past the hint of flirting from her earlier comment.

"I owe much of the substance of my theory to you. It started with the images you described last night." He moved across from her, leaning against a branch that had taken off from the tree at a bizarre angle, a past victim of wind or lightning. "You said last night that the images were memories, but that they weren't yours."

"I actually believed that at the time. They were so vivid, so frightening. But I'm smart enough to know that can't be possible. At least, I hope it can't."

"I think it can."

"Don't patronize me, Clint."

"I wouldn't. Just let me explain. I think the images you saw last night were so real because they're part of the trauma that caused your mind to go into overload and block out the past. I know that's not how a psychiatrist or a neurologist would explain amnesia, but it's how I see it, at least in your situation."

"I was on Glenn Road on Monday night, not in Vietnam."

"Vietnam? You didn't mention Vietnam last night."

"Vietnam." She stood up, a feeble attempt to shake off the confusion that had dropped its impenetrable cloak over her mind again. "I don't know where that came from, Clint. Have I ever been to Vietnam?"

"No. But McCord has. He won the Congressional Medal of Honor for his actions in the heat of battle." Clint reached out and grabbed her hand, tugging her closer so she stood beneath the bare branches of the tree with him.

"It ties into my theory. I think McCord is being threatened by someone or some group because of something that happened in Vietnam. When the threats became too real, he called you and asked you to come down here so that he could enlist your help in getting to the bottom of it."

"Why didn't he just ask for the FBI's official help? Serious threats against a high political figure would warrant that."

"I don't have any answers, except that McCord prides himself on handling his own business. Or maybe he thinks letting the story out will grab too much negative media attention at a time when his name's being bandied about as the next president of the country."

"Okay. Let's see if I have your theory straight. Someone's threatening McCord. He calls on me for unofficial help. I show up. He ditches all of his security men, and we drive out to a deserted spot on Glenn Road so that no one will overhear what he has to tell me. Someone

follows us and seizes upon that opportunity to attack us.
McCord gets away, though bleeding, and I'm left
wounded.''

She shook her head. The pieces didn't fit. ''Why didn't
he just kill me then and there?''

''I'm sure he planned to. Only McCord was his first
priority.''

''So he left me bleeding and wounded.''

''And possibly unconscious. He might even have
thought he'd killed you. Only, before he got back to
make sure you were dead, you came to and wandered
off.''

Darlene guided her fingers to her temples as the familiar nagging pain struck with renewed vengeance. ''So,
if you hadn't shown up when you did, I'd probably be
dead.''

He gathered her in his arms. ''But you're not. You're
here. Safe.''

She looked up, studying the fine lines etched at the
outside corners of Clint's eyes and the deeper ones that
bracketed his drawn mouth. Whatever their past had
been, she owed him a lot in the present.

''Are you ready to go in?'' he asked, his hand riding
her arm in a slow, reassuring movement. ''The rain isn't
going to hold off much longer.''

''In a minute.'' She pressed her mind to make sense
of everything they'd talked about. ''You said your theory
sprung from the wide-awake nightmare I experienced last
night. I still don't see the connection, except that McCord
was in the war.''

''I think McCord related that story to you before the
two of you were attacked. I think you were dealing with
the horror of it when you were ambushed and hit over

the head. When you came to, it had buried itself in some niche of your mind, along with all your other memories.''

The first spray of a chilling mist stung Darlene's face as she considered the possibility that Clint was right. If he was, the country was in big trouble. They were about to elect to the land's highest office a man who'd been party to a murder.

And this man had been her friend, her mentor, a surrogate father, if she believed everything she'd been told. Why else would she have run to answer his call for help? But this was only a theory. A flawed one, she hoped.

''What's our next step, Clint?''

''I've located an old war buddy of McCord's. He's still a close friend, according to Mary. We're paying a call on him this afternoon, right after you get checked over by Dr. Bennigan.''

The mist suddenly intensified into a cold rain.

''Let's make a run for it before we get soaked.'' Clint took her hand, and she sprinted beside him to the house, not slowing until they'd stamped up the stairs and reached the overhang of the porch.

They hadn't run fast enough. Water trickled from her hair and dripped down her neck, and her wet shirt clung to her breasts.

Clint nudged the door with his foot and pulled her inside. ''Get into some dry clothes. I'll build a fire,'' he said, his fingers already fumbling with the buttons on his own wet shirt.

She didn't move to follow suit. The room was already too warm and growing warmer by the second. She watched as his loosened shirt stretched open, revealing dark, thick hairs. He looked up and caught her staring.

A second later, he'd cleared the distance between them.

Chapter Eight

Clint knew he was making a big mistake when he grabbed a towel from the basket of unfolded laundry and wrapped it around Darlene's wet hair. But he'd read the desire in her eyes and it hit him as hard as if she'd thrown her naked body in front of him. He had to touch her. It was killing him not to, even if it was only to soak up the raindrops that were trailing down her face and neck.

He should laugh, tease, make a joke of the two of them dripping all over the floor. But the restraint he had been using for the last few days stretched beyond his limits. His thumbs rode the smooth lines of her neck, from her earlobe down to her shoulders and back again.

The pain of craving what he shouldn't let himself even think about was excruciating. They had been caught in a thunderstorm. She should look drenched and bedraggled. But all he could see was the woman he'd fallen so desperately in love with that long-ago summer.

His gaze fell to the intoxicating swell of her breasts. To the exquisite thrust of her nipples below the clingy wetness of her shirt. He was out of his mind with wanting her, hungry to carry her to his bedroom and make the memories that were driving him over the edge come alive for her. Hard and hurting from wanting her, he trailed his thumbs from her shoulder, tracing the delicate border of her shirt as it dipped into forbidden areas.

Darlene didn't back away. If she had, he might have been able to force himself to stop. Instead, she took his right hand and placed it on her breast. The movement was a statement, an acknowledgment of the need that raged inside her, the same way it did him. Even more, a statement of trust.

His insides turned to mush. His outside, to rock-hard desire. His fingers caressed, rubbing the nipples to soft peaks that strained at the wet cotton of her shirt.

She raised on tiptoe and teased and feathered his lips with hers. But he couldn't play at this, not this time, not with his emotions stemming from a past he'd never laid to rest. He buried his fingers in the hair at the nape of her neck and claimed her lips.

Their breaths mingled, and the saucy sweetness of her, the taste he'd grown drunk on so many times before, left him shaking. She moaned, tiny seductive croonings that sucked away the last vestiges of his control. Finally, she pulled away, inhaling deeply and laying her head on his shoulder.

"I can't play at this, Darlene. If you want me, say so, and I'll deal with the repercussions later. But I won't play tease and run."

"I wasn't playing." Her quick, shallow breaths tripped up her words.

She eased out of the embrace, but not so far away that he didn't still feel the warmth of her breath against his skin. He trailed her arms with his fingers and then clasped her hands.

"I'd like to make love to you. No—" he shook his head, exhaling a long, exasperating breath "—I ache to

make love to you. But I'm not the kind to take advantage
of a woman who doesn't even know who she is.''

"I don't think 'take advantage' is an accurate description, Sheriff. Perhaps you're not the kind of man to give
in to my advances when I have absolutely nothing of my
real self to offer.''

Her honesty touched him and triggered the type of in-
ner smile he didn't know he was capable of these days.
"Whatever," he said, letting go of her hands and stepping backward for one more look at her kiss-swollen lips
and her flushed cheeks. "But I'm also not the kind to
turn down heaven if it's offered. I may be the sheriff,
duty-bound to protect you, but I'm also a man.''

"I noticed." Bending over, she picked up the towel
that had fallen by her feet. She shook it and tossed it to
him, a grin deepening the dimple in her right cheek.
"Boy, did I notice.''

Leaning against the counter, he watched her walk
away. He was a fool, he decided. If he had a grain of
sense where Darlene was concerned, he'd be miserable
right now, sorely repentant for putting his heart on the
line. Again.

Instead, he was crazy with wanting her, school-boy
eager to kiss her again. Under the right circumstances
he'd make love to her, even knowing he'd be all the more
miserable when she left. The people of Vaquero might
think him tough as old jerky, but when it came to Darlene, he was softer than warm butter.

That's why he had to keep his emotions in check.
There was no room for weakness now. Not with McCord
stirring up too much trouble for his small pot. Not with
a would-be murderer on the loose who had his sights set
on Darlene. Not with Darlene on the verge of remem-

bering something that might send the whole country into a tailspin.

James Marshall McCord. *The man of the people.*

Clint fought the knot of apprehension that twisted within him. No matter what he told himself, deep down inside he knew the truth. Knew it even though it cut like a jagged-edged knife. No matter what McCord thought of him, he would put his life on the line for the man, if it came to that.

But, heaven help McCord if he had willingly drawn Darlene into the line of fire. And they might find out the answer to that this afternoon when they visited Jeff Bledsoe, retired Texas Ranger. Bledsoe had been McCord's best friend since the day the senator had lost his left leg saving Bledsoe's life.

But first, they had to make a stop at Dr. Bennigan's office.

DARLENE'S LEGS DANGLED over the edge of the examining table, her feet toasty warm in her boot socks while her arms sported prickly gooseflesh beneath her cotton shirt. "Do you always keep your office this cold?" she asked, rubbing frantically at her arms to produce a little friction heat.

Dr. Bennigan swiveled his stool to get into a better position for removing the stitches from her wound. "Confounded heat's been on the blink for two days." He pushed at the bridge of his eyeglasses.

While the doctor removed her sutures, Darlene's thoughts wandered back to Clint's theory about the connection between what she'd experienced last night and Jim McCord. On the surface, it explained the bizarre images and provided a reasonable explanation. But if she dug much deeper, the theory had serious flaws. It presumed that McCord had told her a gruesome, terrifying war story about men who had broken their bond with humanity, and become as wild and as uncivilized as the jungle they fought in.

And how would McCord know about that episode unless he was there, unless he was part of the deliberate killing of another American soldier?

But those kinds of actions were contrary to everything she'd ever known about McCord. The man had lost a limb saving the lives of his comrades. He'd received the Congressional Medal of Honor. He was a hero, not some drug-crazed warrior.

And he was her friend. If she bought into the theory that McCord was a murderer, what did that say about her?

As always, everything came back to that. Who was she? What was she like?

"Darlene?"

She jerked to attention. The doctor was staring at her, concern pulling his brow into rows of ruddy crevices.

"I'm sorry," she said, sitting up straighter and smiling innocently. "I must have been thinking about something else."

"Not a repeat of the type of images you envisioned last night, I hope."

"No. Nothing like that."

She'd have preferred not to mention that episode to the doctor, but she knew Clint had already discussed it with him. He'd called the doctor last night before they'd left the Altamira, wanting to be sure she was not experiencing a dangerous side effect from the medicines she'd taken at the hospital.

The doctor leaned back and looked at her. "I think it's time you see a psychiatrist, Darlene. I've made an appointment for you with Dr. Fogleman in San Antonio for Wednesday of next week.''

She exhaled slowly, nervously, thrown off guard by the serious tone of his voice. ''Why? Both you and the neurologist said it was likely the amnesia would be temporary.''

''I believed that at first, but sometimes an amnesia patient is responding to more than a physical trauma. I've talked to Dr. Fogleman about your condition. He thinks there's a good chance that's what's happening in your case. It's called hysterical amnesia.''

''You mean, I may be choosing not to remember at all rather than face an unpleasant memory?''

''Something like that. Not consciously, you understand?''

''I'm trying to. I could understand the situation better if the loss of memory was a result of injury. Hysterical amnesia seems so...'' She swallowed hard, hating to face the fact that she had failed everyone—McCord, the sheriff, even herself. ''It seems irresponsible, for lack of a better word.''

''Your amnesia has nothing to do with responsibility, and don't be put off by the term *hysterical*. It simply means the loss is due to an emotionally traumatic event rather than a physical injury. In your case, you had both, making it more difficult at first to determine the source of your memory loss.''

''But I haven't lost all my memory. That's what makes this so strange. I remember countless, routine things. I know how to brush my teeth, wash the dishes, even how to make grilled cheese sandwiches.''

''It's different with every person. In your case, your subconscious seems to be protecting you from something you either can't—or won't—accept.''

He patted her hand. "Look, Darlene, I didn't know you that well, but I treated your grandmother for years. She's a grand lady. I'd be letting her down if I didn't provide you with the best care possible."

"You've done that already, and I appreciate it."

"Then see Dr. Fogleman, Darlene. Once you've dealt with the truth, whatever it is, you'll be able to move past it. You'll be able to handle it. You're made of stern stuff, just like your grandma."

Everything he said made sense, so why was she hesitant to accept his recommendation and visit a psychiatrist? Was her subconscious still protecting her? She scooted off the examining table and thanked Dr. Bennigan. Grabbing her handbag, she hurried down the narrow corridor to the waiting room, where Clint would be drumming his fingers on the arm of the chair and fingering his Stetson impatiently.

He'd be eager to grab a bite to eat and get down to the kind of business he could sink his teeth into: interrogation of a retired Texas Ranger who'd already told Clint he'd be wasting his time by driving all the way to Prairie.

The Ranger didn't want him to come. That in itself assured that Clint would make the trip.

"I'LL TAKE THE CHICKEN Caesar salad," she said, handing the one-page plastic menu to the waitress who was hovering over Clint and batting her huge blue eyes.

"I'll take the cheeseburger, side order of chili fries, extra chili, and a tall glass of milk."

"I'll have it right out, Clint." The waitress smiled and tossed her head, letting her straight blond hair resettle down the middle of her back before she sashayed to the next table. The girl was barely old enough to be out of

high school, but she obviously had a crush on the dashing
cowboy lawman. Now that Darlene thought about it, it
seemed half the eligible females in town did.

"Have you ever been married, Clint?" she asked.

"Where did that question come from?"

"I was just wondering. The females of Vaquero appear
to be lined up and waiting for you to notice them."

"I notice them. All men notice adoring women. It's
our favorite trait in the opposite sex. I'm just discreet in
my appreciation of them."

"And evasive in your responses."

"I've never been married. Are you thinking of proposing?" A smile parted his lips, but his eyes telegraphed
a more serious message. He could never take being with
her lightly, never flirt harmlessly with her the way he did
with every other female in his life.

Warmth flushed her cheeks. What she was thinking of
proposing was better not said in public.

She was saved from responding by the appearance of
a lumbering giant in dark blue slacks and a very un-
western sport shirt, the top buttons of which had been
saved from wear. A triplet of gold chains wrapped his
neck, and dangled over the tattooed head of a lion that
peeked through the dark hairs on his chest. He looked as
out of place in this rural café as if he'd just climbed down
the bean stalk.

"Glad I ran into you, Clint. I tried to find you a while
ago, but Randy said you were driving over to Prairie and
he didn't expect you back until late."

"I'll be heading that way as soon as we finish with
lunch."

The giant hooked a booted foot around the leg of a
chair and joined them without waiting to be asked. The
boots were apparently his only concession to the flavor

of the Lone Star State. "Mary said you'd been asking about me," he said, propping his elbows on the table.

"I did. She told me you were in New York on business."

"Yeah. Spent two days up there. You know how Whitt Emory is. He's the hardest working aide I've ever met. He wants everything ironed out to perfection before the big speech McCord's going to make on New Year's Eve. It's a mistake, if you ask me, trying to provide protection in that madhouse. Looks like the whole country's going to descend on Times Square for the big millennium celebration."

"I hear the demonstrations have already started—people predicting the end of the world."

"You wouldn't believe. They'll have more kooks per square foot than an insane asylum." He smiled at Darlene and readjusted himself in a chair that was way too narrow for him. "And is this pretty lady the Miss Darlene Remington I've been hearing so much about?"

"I'm sorry. I forgot you've never met."

Darlene shook the man's hand as Clint completed the formal introductions, explaining that Bernie Cullen was McCord's personal assistant. A translation for the word *assistant* wasn't necessary. Bernie was the bodyguard she'd heard about, the one who supposedly stuck closer than a shadow to McCord, daring anyone to mess with his boss.

Except for the night they'd been attacked when Bernie had been uncharacteristically missing. And now, when McCord had decided he was better off working alone than surrounded by his personal security staff.

Bernie scanned the small café and then returned his attention to Clint. "Have you got any ideas as to what McCord's up to?"

"Not a clue."

"I don't like it." Bernie shook his head and frowned, his top lip overriding his bottom one. "McCord's a good man, but he still thinks he can take on the world. He forgets he's getting older, that he operates on one good leg. That's why Whitt hired me and told me to stick to him every second."

"So, it was Whitt Emory's idea to hire you?"

"Yeah, and he's on my case big time about letting McCord slip away from me. The man looks after McCord like a son would, if the big man had a son."

"Yeah, if he had a son."

"Only blood kin could reason with a man like McCord once he makes up his mind to do something."

"And what is it you think he's made up his mind to do?"

"Go after whoever attacked him and Miss Remington the other night. Handle the matter his way. Everyone knows that, except maybe Whitt and McCord's niece Robin. They think he's off by himself getting psyched up for the big New Year's Eve speech. They said he'd tried to get them to go with him on a surprise vacation, but they had too much work to do."

The bell at the front door jangled as Freddie Caulder stepped inside. Bernie frowned. "So, Mr. I-Know-Everything does stop for lunch." He turned and looked the other way when Clint acknowledged Caulder with a wave of his hand.

Darlene caught the eye of the bodyguard. "Are you and Freddie Caulder having problems?"

"No more than Caulder has with everyone. He just thinks he runs the Altamira. That's all."

"He does run the ranch," Clint reminded him. "He's

the foreman, and McCord pretty much gives him a free hand when he's away.''

Bernie leaned in closer. "He might run the ranch, but he don't run me. And he don't run Thornton Roberts either. I heard them going at it the other day over the access code for the front gate. Thornton's one of the best security guys in the business—he's got the whole place wired for every contingency. And Freddie Caulder bungles around and sets off alarms almost every day.''

"Sometimes it's hard for old ranchers to get used to high tech," Clint offered.

"Maybe. All the same, Sheriff, Caulder gets huffy when anyone questions McCord's disappearance, and I think that's mighty strange. He doesn't like your coming around asking questions either.''

"So I've been told.''

Darlene joined Clint in saying goodbye to the giant. She watched him stride across the room and take a seat at the long bar. He walked right past Caulder without so much as a nod.

"Looks like more trouble at the Altamira," she said.

The smiling, adoring waitress stopped at their table before Clint had time to respond. "You ought to come out to the Road House Tavern tomorrow night, Sheriff." She leaned low as she set his burger plate on the table. "There's a band out of Austin coming down to play. Everyone says they're good, and they've got a singer sounds just like George Strait.''

"I might have to come out and make sure they're checking IDs. How old are you?''

"Turned twenty-one last week.''

Clint shook his head as she swung her hips and walked away. "There goes trouble.''

"Is the Road House Tavern one of your local hang-outs?"

"My hangout is my ranch. But I've visited the tavern on many a Friday or Saturday night. Always to break up a brawl between a couple of young bucks after the same doe, or to arrest a man who's had a few too many."

They settled into eating. Darlene wondered if she'd ever been to the tavern in question, wondered if any young buck had ever fought over her. If so, she'd probably been as smitten as the waitress was, if Clint had ever come riding to her rescue.

So much about herself she didn't know. So much about everything to do with Vaquero she didn't know.

CLINT SPENT THE FIRST fifteen minutes of the drive on the phone with his deputy, going over facts he'd apparently had Randy digging through databases to recover. He spent the next fifteen chatting with someone in Washington, D.C., trying to pinpoint the exact date of the battle in which McCord had lost his left leg performing acts of heroism.

At first, Darlene had tried to concentrate on what she could hear of the conversation, but her mind had grown numb. She forced her eyes to stay open by studying the passing scenery and searching the bare limbs of trees for species of birds. So far she'd counted seven, including a hawk and a woodpecker—all cast against a backdrop so blue that it might have been painted by a school child with only one color choice in her box of crayons. The clouds from the morning had disappeared without a trace.

Somewhat the way McCord had, except that he'd made phone calls to a select few, telling them not to worry. She was apparently on his "select few" list.

"Isn't anyone except us worried about McCord's

safety?'' she asked, when Clint finally hung up his cell phone. ''I mean, plans are apparently going ahead for his millennium speech in New York. Do you think he's given the go-ahead?''

Clint stretched as far as the cramped cab of his truck would let him and then inhaled slowly, as if weighing his answer. ''I think a lot of people are concerned. They just don't believe he can't handle the situation, or any situation, for that matter. You'd have to know McCord to understand.''

''I do know him.''

''And if you could remember all you know about him, you might be inclined to blow this off as another of his fact-finding missions for which he doesn't want anyone's help.''

''I doubt it. His blood was on my shirt and a scrap of his shirt was in a bush out on Glenn Road.''

''Which doesn't necessarily mean he was seriously injured. The amounts of *his* blood were minimal. Most of the stain was a perfect match with yours. He might have torn his shirt chasing, or hiding from, the attackers.''

''So now he just disappears, makes a few phone calls, and people go on as if nothing were the matter.''

''Apparently he's made more than a few phone calls. He's talked to you, his foreman, his secretary, even a reporter he had an interview scheduled with this morning.''

''What did he tell the secretary and the reporter?''

''That he's taking a break from the media and all their hype, that he needs some time to himself to think things through.''

''But surely you don't believe that.''

''I would, if we didn't have a murderer after you. And

if McCord wasn't so persistent that I drop the investigation."

"Does McCord know someone tried to kill me the other night at the hospital?"

"I haven't told him, but then I haven't had the opportunity to talk to him."

It would have been impossible to mistake the sarcasm in Clint's voice. The better she got to know him, the more convinced she became that he was downplaying the distrust that existed between him and McCord—making light of an issue that sat heavily in his heart, the same way he talked of their having been lovers. As if it were just something that happened, like a disagreement about whether to have steak or chicken for dinner.

She pulled her legs onto the seat and wrapped an arm around her knees, turning to watch Clint's profile as he drove. The truth was, she liked looking at him. Liked the way his cowboy hat topped off the dark locks of hair that were always dancing about his eyebrows. Liked the color of his skin: bronzed from the sun. Liked his nose. Not classic like a Hollywood star, but solid, angular—a real man's nose.

Memories. Somewhere in the ones she'd misplaced, she had shared a relationship with the mysterious sheriff. They'd kissed. They'd made love. But had it been with the same passion they'd drowned in this morning? And if it had, how could she have endured losing him?

Clint swung his visor to the left, blocking out the penetration of the sun. Then he glanced her way. "McCord is worried about you, Darlene. I think you know that. He wants you to go back to Washington. He thinks you'd be safer there. He'll hire protection for you."

"How do you know that?"

"Caulder told me last night."

"Why didn't you mention this earlier?"

"At the time, I thought it would be a mistake. I thought you'd be safer here, where I could watch you. Where you could tell me if you remembered anything, the way you did last night."

"And now?"

"Now I'm not so sure. Maybe it would be better for you if you were in your own place, surrounded by your own things, talking to friends unrelated to the trauma."

Last night he thought she should stay. This afternoon he thought she should leave. But only one thing had changed in the intervening hours. She had spent the night in his house. And they had kissed. One taste of what they'd had before and he was ready to push her out of his life.

If she could remember what had come between them before, what had severed their relationship and killed their love, she might agree with him. She might be running back to D.C. today instead of riding down a straight Texas highway with him at the wheel.

Only she couldn't remember any of that. All she knew was that the taste of him was still on her mouth and that she wanted to kiss him again so badly that she ached.

"I'm staying here, Clint, until everything is settled. Until the killer is apprehended and I know for certain what I witnessed last Monday night."

"You might be making a mistake."

"It probably won't be my first."

She scooted closer, near enough to inhale the musky scent of him. Familiarity draped about her, cocooning her in its embrace. All the facts of their past relationship still eluded her, but the feelings had resurfaced, found a way to escape the darkened dungeons created by amnesia.

Why else would being with Clint seem so right in a world that had gone so wrong?

THE MAN REVVED THE ENGINE of his pickup truck and pulled onto the highway, bound for Prairie, Texas, and Jeff Bledsoe's ranch. How thoughtful of the sheriff to make his task so much easier. A nice isolated, one-man operation.

A quick, effectual strike, and one half of his current mission would be completed. Of course, Clint Richards would probably have to die as well. The plan: take no prisoners.

Too bad. It would have been nice to have a snappy little FBI babe to do his bidding for a while. And he bet she was really good at what she did. At least the sheriff didn't seem to have any complaints.

But too much was riding on the success of this mission. Darlene Remington had to die. And tonight wouldn't be any too soon.

Chapter Nine

Darlene shifted in her seat. The comfort level of the ride had decreased significantly when they pulled onto a bumpy dirt road, but the scenery had remained basically the same. Hilly, tree-dotted pasture edged with rows of barbwire. They had met few vehicles on the Farm-to-Market Road they'd just left, and this one appeared to be considerably more deserted.

"How much farther?" she asked, rummaging in her purse for her sunglasses.

"Another thirty minutes."

"I'd say Jeff Bledsoe isn't bothered by door-to-door salesmen." She pulled out the sunglasses and wiped them with a tissue before settling them on her face. "Does all this land belong to him?"

"No. We have to go through several gates before we drive onto his land. He only has the right of passage through this property. I won't have any trouble finding it, though. A cousin of my dad's owns the land that borders his. I've been out here a time or two when my dad was still alive."

"I know Bledsoe's supposed to be a good friend of McCord's, but how do you know him?"

Clint fingered the brim of his hat, tugging it a little

lower over his forehead. But not so low that a sneaky shock of black hair didn't manage to escape.

"I've handled a few cases with him. He was a Texas Ranger. Worked the area around Vaquero until about five years ago when he lost a good friend and partner to the bullet of a two-bit gang leader. After that, he claimed he lost his taste for the job."

"I can't say that I blame him." Law enforcement, dealing with criminals and their victims every day of your life—it was an odd way to spend one's life. And yet she'd apparently made that same choice. The reasons for her decision were but another facet of her life locked in the hidden recesses of her mind.

Darlene had gotten her exercise, jumping out at each gate, swinging it open and then closing it after Clint had driven through. The one they were approaching now sported a crudely carved sign announcing they'd arrived at the Borrowed Time. The name triggered unsettling feelings.

"This is the beginning of Bledsoe's place," Clint informed her as she yanked the truck door closed behind her. "He said to take the left fork, and we'd be able to see the roof of his house over the tree line."

"Would I have had reason to come out here before, Clint?"

"Possibly, but Bledsoe didn't mention it when I called."

She cupped her hands under her elbows and struggled for a deep breath.

"Are you cold? I could turn the heat on."

"No. It's just a feeling I have, that I've been here before or that I know something about this place."

"A good sign that your memory's on the rebound. I'm

sure you've heard McCord mention his old army buddy Bledsoe before.''

''I guess you're right.''

Only it didn't feel like a good sign. It felt dark and ominous, chilling her clear to the bone. Dr. Bennigan's recommendation that she see a psychiatrist was actually beginning to seem like an excellent idea. She couldn't go on like this, jumping without cause from normalcy to paralyzing fear.

Only there was cause. She'd escaped two attempts on her life in the last few days.

Clint slowed the truck to a stop under a canopy of branches. Apprehension crawled up her spine. ''What is it? Why did we stop?''

With a finger to his lip to quiet her, Clint lowered his window and pointed to a rustle of feathers in the high grass a few yards off the road. Four turkey hens ignored them and went about their foraging.

Her trepidation dissolved in a flurry of pleasure. ''They're not afraid of us at all,'' she whispered in a voice low enough not to spook the fascinating creatures. ''Are they pets?''

''No, they're wild, but no one bothers them out here. They think they own the place. Still, they'd run for cover if you walked toward them.''

Clint indulged her delight for a few more seconds and then eased the truck back into gear and slowly rounded the next curve. The house came into full view at that point, a rambling one-story that looked as if it had withstood the ravages of decades of changing seasons.

A railed porch ran across the entire front, the landing spot for a couple of rocking chairs, an aluminum table and a long-haired cat who had claimed the top of a foam cooler.

Darlene steeled her nerves for what was to come as Clint descended the hilly drive and parked behind a black pickup. Clint expected her to rehash the images that had tormented her last night at the Altamira, give Bledsoe all the gory details, and then see if he recognized them as an experience McCord had shared with him either in grisly, living color or in conversation.

If he did, they would know the events were not an unrelated hallucination, but part of the truth Darlene had learned, part of the horror that had shut down a vital part of her mind and left her a stranger in her own body.

The only redemption in such a revelation would be that they would gain insight into the events surrounding Monday night's attack. Looking for the guilty parties would be less a stab in the dark and more of a process of elimination, if they knew what McCord had told her that last time they'd been together.

If the waking nightmare of the other night was actually a memory from McCord's life, perhaps Bledsoe could tell them who from that scenario might be seeking revenge thirty years after the fact.

By the time Clint had parked the truck and they had started up the steps, she was shaking. He laid a reassuring hand at the small of her back. "I wish there were another way to do this, Darlene, but it'll be better if the images you saw the other night come from you. The details will be sharper, and you might even remember more of them once you start talking."

The prospect of pulling out the horror again and sharing it with a stranger strained her control. "An FBI agent with weak knees and a cowardly heart. My supervisor must love me."

"Cut yourself a little slack. FBI agents aren't usually

investigating their own attempted murder or the mysterious disappearance of a longtime friend.''

"I'll try to remember that on my next case, if there
ever is a next case.''

He dropped his right hand from her back and used it
to knock on the door. The gray cat took that as her sum-
mons and jumped from the cooler, padding across the
bare planks of the porch to wrap herself around Darlene's
ankle.

She bent and dipped her fingers into the luxurious fur
of the cat, sliding them along the slightly arched curve
of her back. *Wish me luck, cat. Or give me one of your
nine lives to save until I need it. The third time might
just be the charm for my would-be assassin.*

THE CAT HAD STAYED curled up on the couch beside Darlene while she'd recounted her story. But the temperature
of the room had taken a sudden downward spiral in the
last few seconds, and the cat had better sense than to stay
for a demonstration of her master's cold anger. She
pounced from the couch to the floor and raced into the
calmer climate of the kitchen.

Darlene doubted she had that option. She scooted to
the back of the couch, amazed at the change that had
come over Jeff Bledsoe as she'd reached the end of her
tale.

"I'm mortified that you put Darlene through this,
Clint. You, of all people.'' Bledsoe narrowed his eyes
and squared his shoulders, his stance and steel-gray eyes
conveying belligerence. "That story Darlene told is
groundless, and you should know that. McCord would
never have been a willing guest at a hanging party.''

"Maybe he wasn't willing.'' Clint didn't back down
to Bledsoe. Neither did he adopt the man's fury. His

voice was calm, steady. "Maybe McCord was just there. A lot of brutal villainies occurred in Vietnam."

"I'm not saying they didn't. But if Jim McCord had witnessed anything even remotely similar to what Darlene described, he would have sought out justice long ago. The man sacrificed a leg in that war. Saved my life and a handful of others. Now you're ready to buy into this damnable lie just because a woman who can't even remember who she slept with last had a vision?"

Darlene bristled. Yet, she couldn't argue the point of it.

"Who Darlene has or hasn't slept with isn't an issue here," Clint stated, scooting to the edge of his chair. "What happened to her Monday night in the company of McCord is."

Bledsoe shrugged. "I'm sorry, Darlene. I didn't mean for my tirade to offend you. I know you can't help what goes on in your mind after you've been hit on the head, but I expect a damn sight more from Clint. He's an officer of the law."

Clint ignored him. "So, let me get this straight, Bledsoe. Are you telling me that you have never heard McCord speak of an incident in which someone in his troop was murdered by one of his fellow soldiers while a small group of his buddies watched?"

"I think I've made that plain enough for a blind man to see."

Clint sauntered over to the kitchen door and leaned against the door frame. "That's plain enough for me." His lips split into a friendly smile. "I'm not out to do McCord harm. I'm just looking for answers. And trying to stop a killing."

Clint's refusal to fly to the defense had taken the steam

out of Bledsoe's anger. Darlene watched the good sheriff at work. He was good. She could learn something here.

"Have you heard from the senator in the last few days?" Clint's tone stayed friendly, as if he were making idle conversation.

Bledsoe scratched his chin and then jammed both hands deep into the pockets of his jeans, rocking forward to the toes of his scuffed boots. "I haven't seen him since this trouble came up. Matter of fact, I haven't seen him in a month of Sundays. He's busy courting the nation's favor. I fully expect him to be the next president of the United States. Unless people start filling the press with the kind of crap you and Darlene are spouting."

Still frowning his displeasure, Bledsoe picked up the beer he'd been nursing ever since they'd arrived and finished it off, holding his head back and giving his Adam's apple a full workout. Bending, he sat the empty can on the boot-scarred edge of his coffee table. "I can't imagine why he'd want to be president, but then I could never imagine him running for the Senate either, and he's been the best thing that happened to Texas since Santa Anna got run off."

"I hope he makes it to the election, Bledsoe. I hate to say it, but I think he's going to have to walk over a madman first, the one who attacked him and Darlene. I'd like to help McCord with this, but I can't find a starting place."

Bledsoe shuffled his feet and diverted his gaze to the floor. "I'd help you out if I could, Sheriff. You know that."

"I'd like to think you would. I'd like to think you'd care more about helping McCord than about keeping a boyish pledge of secrecy. Especially if it meant saving Darlene's life and maybe McCord's as well."

Bledsoe paced the floor. "I don't know anything, Clint. I'd help if I could, but I don't know anything." He stopped his pacing abruptly and looked at Clint. "No," he said, "that's not quite true. I'm going against my word to tell you this, but I know someone's after him. He was shot Monday night. Just a flesh wound, but now he's a man obsessed."

"Does he know who shot him or why?"

"No, but he's working on finding the answer to both of those questions. That's all I know. He called last night to tell me he was safe and that the gunshot wound was healing, but he wouldn't even tell me where he was." Bledsoe turned to Darlene. "That's all I know. I'm sorry I can't help you any more than that."

"You can only tell what you know. But I'm glad you did that much." Clint's gaze swept the kitchen. "Darlene and I might as well be on our way then. No use wasting your time. Mind if I use your bathroom first?"

"Help yourself. It's down the hall."

A few minutes later, Bledsoe excused himself and walked into the kitchen. Darlene walked to the front door and opened it. Her friend Cat was waiting for her. Evidently he had an escape hatch from the kitchen.

She stepped onto the porch. Cat disappeared under the front steps for a second and then came out with something in his mouth. He crept over and dropped his prized gift at her feet: a dead rat.

Her stomach lurched. "No wonder you're so fat," she scolded.

Cat nudged the rat in her direction. Darlene looked around and spotted an old cardboard box in the corner of the porch. She tore off a piece of the corrugated material and made a scoop. Avoiding any contact with the rat, she dipped it up and headed to the trash barrel at the side of the house. She elbowed the top off and dumped Cat's prize—

Her heart plummeted to her stomach. Buried near the bottom of the barrel was a piece of fabric exactly like the one she and Clint had found stuck in the brush out on Glenn Road. Exactly like the shirt McCord had been wearing on the afternoon of the attack.

She was about to dig the cloth from the leftover food and debris when the screen door squeaked open. She jumped away from the can, hoping Bledsoe wouldn't notice what she'd been doing. Faking an air of nonchalance, she strolled toward them.

"Looking for something, Darlene?" Bledsoe's voice was edgy.

"No. Just disposing your cat's ratty lunch." She said goodbye, all but bursting with the news she had to share with Clint as soon as they were out of Bledsoe's hearing range.

If that piece of fabric was actually McCord's shirt, then Bledsoe had been lying through his teeth about not having seen his good buddy since the attack. And if he lied about that, he could be lying about everything.

The second Clint pulled away she burst into a detailed account of her find. She'd expected him to show a little excitement, or at least tell her what a great job she'd done. But his expression never changed.

"I take it you don't think that was McCord's shirt."

"Oh, I don't doubt it was his shirt. McCord probably showed up here the night of the attack for first aid. Truth is, he probably called Bledsoe to come and pick him up. I could kick myself from here to Austin that I didn't come looking for him here then."

"All the same, we need to retrieve that shirt. You go back in, make some kind of excuse, like you forgot something. While you keep him talking, I'll dig the shirt out of the trash can.''

He accelerated, hitting a bump in the road and knocking her toward him. She straightened up fast.

''So you're not even going to check out the shirt?'' she complained.

''What will it prove, except that McCord's been there? He isn't there now.''

''What makes you so sure?''

''The dishes.''

Exasperated, she exhaled a slow breath, a common habit now that she'd started hanging with the sheriff. ''Explain yourself.''

''Bledsoe's dinner dishes were in the sink. One plate, one glass, one fork.''

''Maybe he outsmarted you. He could have washed McCord's dishes.''

''Possibly, but the bathroom had only one towel hanging on the rack and only one wet cloth.''

''That still doesn't guarantee McCord isn't around. I think we should sneak back, hide in the brush and watch the house.''

''How long do you recommend we sit out in the dark watching?''

''All night if we have to.''

''A stake-out in the dark sounds intriguing, but it's not in your job description as a witness in protective custody.''

''You know, Sheriff, I'm not just your ordinary civilian victim. I'm an FBI agent. I may not remember whom I slept with last—as Bledsoe so crudely pointed out—but that doesn't mean I'm not a trained agent. I can call the Bureau and request this investigation be given top priority, and I just may do that. Have this case yanked right out of your hands. We're talking about a U.S. senator, you know.''

The authority in her voice surprised even her. Her memory might or might not be returning, but she was getting some spunk, showing a little Texas grit. Maybe her real personality was beginning to surface.

She turned her full attention to Clint. He was finally displaying a little emotion—the wrong emotion. His eyes were dancing, and his lips curved in that crooked, heart-stopping smile he had perfected to sinful levels. She refused to be charmed.

''I think you should assign someone to watch the house and make sure McCord doesn't show up here. If he does, you can apprehend him and demand he tell you what's going on.''

He laughed out loud, and she realized it was the first time she'd heard him really laugh. The sound was seductively masculine, deep and intriguing. He slowed the truck and stopped, right in the middle of the deserted road. Circling her shoulder with his right hand, he tugged her closer.

''Welcome back, Darlene.''

He tucked a thumb under her chin and lifted, holding her face inches from his. Her breath caught. She couldn't be charmed? What a crock. She was so charmed that parts of her body—ones she had no idea were even erogenous—were trembling in anticipation. She waited for what seemed an eternity before he finally touched his lips to hers....

The kiss was hot, hungry and over all too fast. He pulled his mouth away and brushed an errant strand of hair from her cheek, tucking it behind her ear. ''I think we better get out of here while we still can,'' he said.

''You should have told me that asserting myself with

you is such an aphrodisiac. I might have tried it sooner. And, by the way, I still think I'm right about having someone do a stakeout at Bledsoe's, just to make certain McCord or even the killer doesn't show up out here."

"I agree. And I'll have someone on it right away. But you're not that someone."

He drove another quarter-mile before turning the truck off the road and circling back toward the area they'd just left.

"Where are you going now?"

"To a spot where I can watch Bledsoe's house and determine the best opportunity to sneak through the brush and raid his garbage can."

"So you're not going to just drive off and leave the shirt."

"Of course not."

"Then why didn't you let me go back and get it?"

"I hate to be outdone by an FBI agent—a female one at that."

He was teasing, of course. He was doing it this way because it was smarter than her way. She could see that now. He hadn't wanted Bledsoe to suspect she'd seen anything she shouldn't, so he'd kept a poker face while she'd talked in the driveway and then driven far enough that if Bledsoe was watching, he'd believe they were headed back to town.

He had bettered her. Still, she found herself smiling. In spite of his insistence that there was no "we" in this investigation, they were almost a team.

Strange, but she had been born again Monday evening. All memories left behind, she'd entered into a world of frightening shadows where murderers lurked around dark corners. And yet right now, she couldn't imagine that she

would rather be anywhere else in the world than sitting
in the cab of Sheriff Clint Richards's pickup.

THE GARBAGE HEIST went off without a hitch. And the
garment was indeed McCord's. One sleeve was ripped
off. Bloodstains splattered the other sleeve and the front
of the garment.

The bloody piece of evidence was now stashed behind
the seat of the truck, in the same spot where Clint had
stashed the gun he'd given her to hold when he'd gone
to pillage Bledsoe's garbage.

The mystery of who shot the senator was heating up,
but no closer to being solved. Like Darlene's memory,
McCord was elusive and enigmatic. A puzzle that defied
completion.

The only positive thing in her life right now was the
sheriff—a man who obviously wanted her and yet
couldn't, or wouldn't, let himself give in to that need.
Yet every second she was with him, she felt more entan-
gled in the relationship they must have shared.

Even now her memories of him were riding so close
to the surface that she could all but taste them. They must
have driven like this before, alone in his truck with the
first stars of the evening glittering through the trees, and
silvery moonbeams dancing in the air like fireflies.

She closed her eyes and let her thoughts ramble, hoping they'd return to a time when she and Clint had been
years younger, and when the constant threat of a murderer had not hung over them. A young couple newly in
love, kissing the way they'd kissed this morning. His
touch searing her flesh the way it had done through the
thin wet fabric of her shirt when the rain had sent them
scurrying for shelter.

The attraction she felt for Clint was so strong, and yet

she knew it hadn't all developed this week. The feelings between them were new but they touched something of the past, a silken cord of desire that had tied them together in the past.

And now Clint wanted her to walk out of his life again, to fly back to Washington and renew a life that didn't include him. To give up on them.

She touched his arm. "I've been thinking about what you said earlier, Clint, about my flying back to Washington."

"We'll talk about it later."

"There's no need. My mind's made up. My memories were lost here, and this is where they'll resurface. Whatever happened involves the people of this town, especially McCord. If necessary, I'll ask Mary if I can stay at the Altamira."

"The Altamira?" His muscles grew tense and hard beneath her hand. "Still McCord's girl—and you don't even remember the man."

His words took her by surprise; they were so bitter that they hit her like a slap to the face. She rode in silence until the truck jerked to a stop at the gate to exit Borrowed Time.

"I'll get it this time," Clint said. "You've had a long day."

She lay her head against the back of the seat and closed her eyes. She was tired, not so much from the visit to Bledsoe as from the confrontation with Clint. Every time she thought she was beginning to understand him, another facet of his personality surfaced and left her staggering in its wake.

The rusty hinges of the gate squeaked open. She glanced up just in time to see a man on horseback step from the overhanging branches of a sycamore tree, the moon glinting off a rifle he held in his right hand.

Chapter Ten

One minute Darlene was trembling, paralyzed with fear; the next she was hanging over the back of the truck seat, stretching to reach the revolver. Her mind gyrated in panic, but her reflexes were those of a robot who'd been programmed by a higher order.

Gun in hand, finger on the trigger, she shoved the door open and jumped to the hard ground. "Come any closer, and I'll shoot."

Clint spun around, losing his hold on the gate. It swung back into place with an ear-shattering *clang*. The gunman stopped a good twenty yards away from them, sitting high in his saddle but holding the rifle away from his body and waving his left hand above his head in surrender.

"Drop the gun," she ordered with authority. She had no idea the words were going to come out of her mouth until they'd spiked the cool night air.

"Mind if I just slide it into its holster? Darn thing's liable to go off if I drop it. Liable to spook my horse as well, and I'm not looking to get thrown."

"Make it slow and easy. Then ride in closer with your hands where I can see them."

"Yes, ma'am. I wouldn't want to rile a lady with a loaded weapon."

The man rode in a few yards closer, whistling. It was to keep her from losing her cool, she suspected, though it wasn't working. Her trigger finger was steady, but inside she was shaking so viciously she was afraid she was going to be sick. She turned to Clint, but he was silent, just standing back near the gate and watching her, a crooked smile tugging at the corners of his lips.

The truth seeped in slowly. The man riding toward them wasn't a stranger to him. He hadn't planned on gunning them down and leaving their bodies for the buzzards. The breath she'd unknowingly been holding rushed from her lungs in a deflating *whoosh*.

"What the Sam Hill?" the man said when he was close enough to speak to them without raising his voice. He spit a stream of something grungy on the ground, and turned to get a better look. "You haven't gone and gotten yourself some female gun-toting deputy, have you, Clint?"

"No, but I might, if she's applying for the job. She sure put the skids on your reins."

"I thought you were…" She quit talking, shaking her head in exasperation when the explanation on the tip of her tongue grew too burdensome.

"Don't worry, Darlene." Clint stepped in closer, his body profiled in the twin beams of light from the truck. "You have every reason to be jumpy." He took the gun from her. "If I hadn't recognized my dad's cousin Leon, I'd have pulled my gun on him too. Knowing him like I do, it still isn't a half-bad idea."

The older man laughed, but his faced tensed as if he didn't really find the statement funny. "You wouldn't have been the first guy today to pull that stunt."

"Yeah?" Clint stepped in closer. "I thought you gave up chasing skirts years ago. What'd you do to get in trouble now?"

The man twisted in his saddle, checking the open pasture to the north and the wooded area to the west before turning back to Clint. "I caught some fool hunter trespassing. Told him to hightail it off my land unless he had a printed invitation, and I hadn't mailed any out. He smarted off right back at me, and then out of nowhere just reared back and pulled a pistol on me."

"Looks like you talked him out of using it."

Leon chuckled nervously. "Not before I swallowed a choking wad of tobacco. The man had me scared as a struttin' rooster when the preacher comes a-calling. He backed down, though, when I told him a buck's rack on his wall wasn't worth spending his life in prison."

Clint propped a foot on the front bumper of his truck. "Mighty aggressive behavior for a Bambi slayer."

"That's the reason I rode back out here tonight, just to see if the man was hanging around out here somewhere. I don't go looking for trouble, but I get in a tail-kickin' mood when someone pulls a gun on me, especially on my side of the fence."

"Do you have any idea who he was?"

"No one I'd ever seen before. That's why I figured him for a hunter. One of those city guys that thinks posted signs are part of the landscape and everything on four legs is wild game. I had a young steer shot last year by a guy down here from the Midwest. At least he had the decency to fess up, though."

Clint walked around to the driver's side of the truck. Reaching in, he flicked the key in the truck's ignition, killing the engine. The silence that followed darkened the mood as quickly as Darlene's actions had stopped the cowboy a minute ago.

"Can you describe this man?" Clint asked, stepping back to the front of the truck and leaning on the fender nearest Darlene.

Leon climbed down from his horse and looped the reins over one of the gateposts. "Why do I get the feeling your interest's been roused by more than my tale of a trespassing hunter? There's not some escaped convict loose in these parts, is there? If there is, I have a right to know. I have a wife to protect."

"No escaped convict that I know of."

Leon buried his fingers in his back pockets, the stance adding a little dimension to his scrawny chest. He was tall, wiry, with thin hair as silvery as the moon that reflected off it. "So, what brought you out to see Jeff Bledsoe?"

"A little trouble back in Vaquero. I thought Bledsoe might know something. He didn't."

"Nothing serious, I hope."

Serious as death. The thought bore into Darlene's brain, but she didn't say it. She just sucked in a breath as she felt again the all-too-familiar tightening in her chest.

"What kind of trouble you chasing down?" Leon asked, when Clint didn't offer any further elaboration.

Clint lay a hand on Darlene's shoulder. "My would-be deputy here is Darlene Remington. She was visiting in Vaquero when someone ambushed her a few nights ago, a few miles out of town. We're looking to find out who did it."

Leon directed his gaze toward Darlene. "No wonder you were so quick on the draw tonight." He stepped closer, his face acquiring new and deeper worry lines as he squinted to get a better look at the bandage on her head. "Looks like you took quite a blow."

Darlene shook her head. "It's all right now. I'm just looking for answers as to why I was the chosen victim." She was aware that Clint hadn't mentioned her connection with McCord, or that her attacker had tried to kill her while she lay in a hospital bed. She followed suit, giving out as few of the details as possible.

Leon rocked back on his heels, his expression indicating he wasn't completely buying their story. "I still don't get it," he said. "What brought you to Prairie? And why are you so interested in the man I had the run-in with?"

"I just wanted to check out some possibilities with Jeff," Clint explained, keeping his voice level and reassuring. "He has a good head for this sort of thing."

"He was in the business long enough."

"I still need a description of the hunter," Clint insisted.

Leon looked Clint square in the eye. "You're thinking the man was out here to ambush the two of you, aren't you?"

"It could be."

Leon took off his hat and slapped it against his leg. "You're damn right. And that makes a lot more sense, now that I think about it. He had his truck parked behind that clump of brush just over there." Leon pointed to a cluster of overgrown bushes with a couple of cacti spiking out of the middle. "All he had to do was stay out of sight until you came by on your way back from Bledsoe's and stopped to open the gate."

Darlene shuddered, the hard truth sinking into her mind. The man who'd cracked open her head and stolen her memories, the man who'd been in her hospital room, who'd had his hands around her neck, squeezing away her life, had been in this very spot—waiting for them.

"You'd have been a sitting duck, Clint." Leon let out a low whistle and a string of mild curses.

"We're dealing with speculation, Leon."

"Speculation, my ass. 'Scuse me, Miss Darlene. But this burns me up one side and down the other. He was probably expecting you to be the one to get out and open that gate. He'd have shot you down like a dog, and then all he had to do was take out a couple of Clint's tires. He would have taken off in his truck, and you would never have been able to catch him."

"You're letting your imagination run away with you, Leon."

"No, I don't think so." The rancher yanked a bandanna from his back pocket and swiped it across his brow, gathering a row of moisture that had popped out like measles. "I should have shot the man on the spot. Do you think he'll come back? I'm not afraid for me, but I've got my family to think about."

Darlene read the fear in his eyes, understood it, even felt the chill of it. Murders were in the news every day, commonplace occurrences. And yet, when it came so near you could smell the vileness, it took on new dimensions of terror.

"I don't think you need to worry, Leon. This isn't a serial killer, at least I don't think he is. He's just trying to make sure Darlene doesn't live to tell what she knows or to identify him."

"And now I could identify him. Who's to say he's not going to come after me?"

"You'd only be identifying a trespasser. As long as he doesn't know you've talked to me, he won't imagine you have a clue as to what he was really doing here. And even now we can't be sure it's the same man.''

Leon looked around, his eyes round and alert, his hands clenching and unclenching in a nervous rhythm. ''I need to get back to the house.''

''In a minute, Leon. Just describe the man. Then I'll ride back with you if you'd like.''

''No, I'll describe him as best I can, but then you just go on ahead. I don't want any dealings with a killer, and I don't want him thinking I told you anything.''

''Start with his approximate height and weight,'' Clint said, his voice steady, his tone all business. ''Then just describe any details you can remember. Hair color, skin color, identifying marks.''

Darlene listened to every word, trying to paint a picture of the man with the few sketchy details Leon offered. Middle-aged, graying, around six feet. When Clint was finally convinced that he couldn't pull any distinctive identifying details out of Leon's choppy memory, he opened the passenger door for Darlene.

''And you really believe this man won't come back after me?'' Leon asked, sliding his right foot into the stirrup.

''If he'd wanted to kill you, Leon, you'd already be dead.''

''You got a rotten sense of humor, you know that, Clint?'' Leon tipped his hat to the two of them and yanked the reins, heading back in the direction he'd come. He twisted around to face them for one parting shot. ''Watch out for him, Darlene. That badge he wears don't cover his heart. It *is* his heart.''

Leon meant it as a joke, and Clint laughed it off appropriately. So why did she have the sinking feeling that Leon was more right than he guessed?

Maybe because Clint had already climbed back into the state of deep concentration he was so good at, shutting her out, even though he had to know how welcome his arm would be around her shoulder, had to know that her insides quaked and that her heart was pounding against the walls of her chest.

There was a good chance she was alive tonight as a result of a rancher riding his fence line on a cool day with nothing more to bother him than whether he should check out the north pasture or the west one.

But the killer was still out there, apparently growing more desperate by the minute. He knew who she was, and apparently she knew who he was as well. Except that her knowledge had sunk into a black abyss of forgetfulness, and no amount of determination on her part could bring it back.

"Damn James McCord!"

Darlene snapped to attention as Clint's curse echoed through the cab of the truck.

"This may not be his fault, Clint."

"Oh, it's his fault, all right. And I'll find out exactly how before it's all over. In the meantime, he's right."

"About what?"

"The fact that you can't stay here. I can't protect you—not against this. You'll have to go back to Washington, let the big man buy you all the guards you need. He's the one you've always turned to. Why should this be any different?"

"Whether or not I go back to Washington is my decision. Not yours and not the senator's."

"Not anymore."

Fury, fear, fatigue. The deadly three raged and collided inside Darlene, but she didn't even try to argue with Clint. The decision was etched into his face, registered in the strain of his voice, meted out by the precision hammering of his fist against the steering wheel.

His mind was made up. But so was hers. She didn't know what she'd been in the past, but the Darlene Remington of here and now was no quitter. Like it or not, Clint Richards was not getting rid of her that easily.

Not this time.

CLINT SLAMMED THE DOOR of his truck and stamped up the steps to his house. Last night he'd gotten nothing of substance from Bledsoe. Now he'd just wound down another day of questioning that had gotten him nowhere. Freddie Caulder claimed he hadn't heard from McCord since the conversation in which the senator had instructed Darlene to go back to D.C. and had ordered Clint to back off.

Bernie the Watchdog was more interested in running back and forth to New York than in finding where the senator had run off to for his dubious vacation. And top-security hound Thornton Roberts didn't seem to have a clue about anything. Not that Clint blamed Thornton for that. It was common knowledge that McCord hired security men for his family, not for himself.

Everything boiled down to James Marshall McCord. Everybody's hero.

Only he wasn't. Not in Clint's eyes. Not since the day he'd learned the truth about him. From hero to villain in one heartbreaking moment of truth. A deathbed confession had finally let Clint see McCord's true colors.

He'd spent the biggest part of his life looking up to the man, emulating everything about him. The way he wore his hat, the way he stood so straight and tall in his saddle when he rode in the Fourth of July parade, the way he swaggered into a group of men and took over the conversation.

When McCord had spoken to their sixth-grade class about patriotism and what they should feel when they said the Pledge of Allegiance to the flag, Clint had even wished he had a false leg, had pretended it had been he who marched into battle and rescued his friends.

The old memories chewed at him now, the way they had so frequently over the last few days. He walked through the empty house straight for the fridge, grabbing a beer and twisting off the cap. McCord was out there now, searching for a killer, sure he didn't need anyone or anything to help him. Most of all, he didn't need the two-bit sheriff from Vaquero, Texas.

Clint leaned against the kitchen counter and took a drought-quenching swig of his beer. The house was quiet, and painfully empty, bathed in the slippery grayness of twilight. A week ago he'd loved coming home at the end of the day. Loved the fact that he answered to no one, that he could put his feet where he wanted and eat cold pizza in front of the TV if that's what he chose.

Tonight, all he felt was alone. He could blame that on McCord too. He had swept Darlene up in his own dilemma, sucked her into danger and then dropped her back into Clint's life. Not for keeps. Just long enough to slash open the jagged scar where his heart had never fully healed. Just long enough to make him ache with the need for her, knowing that if he gave in, the days and weeks after she left would be all the more excruciating for having made love with her.

He finished his beer and tossed the can into the trash, grabbing another before pushing through the back door. Randy had driven Darlene into town to pick up some groceries, and they would be driving up any minute. He had to steer his thoughts back into safer pastures before they arrived, reapply the veneer that would allow him to talk to her about her thoughts and memories while masking all his own.

Most of all, he had to get through one more night without giving in to the urges that were driving him over the edge. She was all too willing. He had seen the desire in her eyes when she looked at him, had felt it in the way her heart beat against his chest when he lost control and held her close. Hell, he had even tasted the passion on her lips.

Only it wasn't really him she wanted. She didn't even know him. She was infatuated by the cowboy who'd saved her. A temporary hero to last until her memory returned and she could resume her job as FBI Agent Darlene Remington, woman of steel. If he had any doubts about that, they'd been dispelled last night when she'd pulled the gun and started cracking orders.

The job was in her blood. He couldn't fault her for that. Texas was in his. Ranching and sheriffing were the only life he knew, the only life he wanted to know. So, he and Darlene were exactly back to where they'd been six years ago—only he'd grown older and wiser. He wasn't signing up for the kind of punishment loving her could dish out. Not again.

Needing the sting of the wind in his face and the smell of cattle and dust in his nostrils, he started walking. He didn't have a destination in mind, nor much of a purpose. He knew only that he needed to push his body to total exhaustion before he faced Darlene. And that even that wouldn't kill the desire that would erupt inside him the second she walked through his door.

"THAT'S CLINT'S TRUCK, so he has to be around here somewhere," Randy announced as he yanked open the back screen door and waited for Darlene to enter in front of him. "Probably took one of the horses out for some exercise, or else he went to check on his cattle in the north pasture."

Darlene flipped the light switch and flooded the kitchen with two hundred watts of power. She'd psyched herself up on the way home to have it out with Clint, to demand to know the truth about what had happened between them six years ago. If she had done some horrible, unforgivable deed in her pre-amnesia life that made it impossible for them to get together or even to be friends, it would be far better for him to just spit out the truth. Especially now that the memory loss was threatening to hang on indefinitely.

Regardless of his comment about their having shared a harmless summer fling, his actions indicated there was more to their past relationship. And call it intuition, a memory breakthrough or just a guess, but she couldn't help believing that whatever had torn them apart had something to do with his bitter feelings toward James McCord.

She walked to the window and stared into the gathering darkness. Loopy lay on the back porch, chewing a dry bone while he swished his tail at a bothersome fly. A squirrel scampered down the trunk of a tree and then back up again as if hurrying to get his aerobic exercise in before the encroaching darkness ended his day. Brandy was necking with a stately bay in the corral. All peaceful.

And this was the way Clint lived. By day he was a lawman who chased the bad guys with a vengeance. On his own time, he was a rancher who liked his horses spirited, his dog loyal, his freedom unquestioned.

She caught a glimpse of him as he stepped inside the

barn that sat a hundred yards or more behind the house. As good a place as any to talk.

Randy stuck his head in the refrigerator. "It's Miller time," he announced, pulling out a beer. "Want one?"

"Might as well."

Randy opened it for her, and she took a sip. She wasn't much of a beer fan, but it had been a long day. "I saw Clint step into the barn, Randy. I think I'll go out and meet him. That way, you can go home and have supper with your family."

"I might just take you up on that. Only, I won't be eating with the folks tonight. I've got a date with a certain little redheaded nurse. We're going to Rosita's to see if we can catch a little heartburn." He winked and smiled.

"No wonder you're in such a good mood."

"Yep. Surprised the heck out of me when she accepted my invitation. Let me grab my jacket, and I'll walk out with you."

"I'd rather go alone and surprise Clint."

He grinned sheepishly. "Sounds like an interesting surprise, but that would be against orders. I'm not supposed to leave until I've officially turned the guard duty over to Clint."

"Then stay at the window and watch. When I get to the barn, I'll wave."

He frowned, but relented. "I guess that would be all right. But don't wave until you actually see Clint. And tell him this was all your idea. He's not much on surprises. And he's way big on following the rules to the letter. Especially where you're concerned."

"So I've noticed." She swung open the back door. "I promise. I won't wave until I see the whites of his eyes."

The paraphrased quote clearly sailed over Randy's

head, but he grinned anyway and stepped over to the window so he could watch for her signal.

"Have fun tonight," she called, slipping out the door and down the steps. She walked quickly, anxious not to let her resolve to confront Clint wither. Loopy followed behind her—yet another guard. He nosed her leg as she walked, and she bent to scratch his head.

A gust of cold wind whipped her hair into her face and cut through the thin cotton of her shirt. She should have taken time to grab a sweater. December evenings in the Hill Country could be biting even when the day had been shirtsleeve warm. Head down, she ran the last few steps to the barn.

"Clint." Her call was soft, tentative. "Clint? Are you in here? I need to talk to you." Her voice echoed, rolling and bouncing off the roof and the wooden beams over her head. The door squeaked shut behind her, the whine of the rusty hinges ragging her already shaky nerves.

"Are you looking for me?"

She jumped as Clint answered, expecting him and yet startled when his voice seemed to come from nowhere. Her eyes adjusting to the twilight gray of the barn, she turned slowly, inspecting each shadowy corner until she spied him leaning against a wooden corner beam. His hat was low on his forehead, a pair of work gloves on his hands, his shirt open at the collar. Her breath caught at the sheer virility of the cowboy in his element.

"I saw you walk into the barn a few minutes ago, and I wanted to talk to you."

"Where's Randy?"

She made a face and groaned. "He's at the house, waiting for me to signal I hooked up with you." Before she had a chance to remedy her mistake, Randy pushed through the door, breathing hard and fast from the speed he'd traveled to get there.

She spread her hands. "I'm sorry, Randy. I forgot, and I can't even blame amnesia this time."

He looked to first one and then the other of them, his expression questioning what might be going on between them. "I didn't mean to bust in on anything. But you didn't signal like you promised, and when that door blew shut, I feared something was wrong."

"Nothing's wrong." Clint stepped out of the shadows and walked over to stand next to Randy. "I'll take over from here, but give me a call first thing in the morning. Reverend Goolsby's yelling for the law to show up and corral those reprobate high-school boys who've been using the church ball field during services. I guess you ought to go over and run them off."

"I'll do it. Quote them a couple of scriptures and a couple of ordinances. If that don't work, I'll threaten to call their mommas."

"Good. Bernie has agreed to drive Darlene to the airport in San Antonio. She has a ten-twenty flight out. As per McCord's request, Emory already has a team lined up to protect her once she gets to D.C."

Irritation clawed its way along Darlene's nerve endings. "Why wasn't I informed of this?"

Clint kicked at a loose pile of hay. "You just were."

"Did you have any luck today?" Randy asked, hedging any personal involvement in the argument brewing around him. "Anything turn up?"

"Nothing of consequence. Mary called McCord's daughter Levi out in Montana, and got permission for me to go through her grandmother's private records. Apparently she kept every letter McCord ever wrote her and every newspaper clipping that's ever carried his name."

Darlene wandered toward the back of the hay-strewn barn as the two men finished their conversation, turning back only to acknowledge Randy's departure. High-school boys desecrating on the Sabbath. A murderer somehow connected with a political figure of national prominence. The chasm that split the two acts seemed as wide as the Atlantic Ocean, and yet they were all in a day's work for Clint.

Perhaps that's all she was too: part of his work. A past lover who fell back into his life. A kiss or two, a helping of renewed passion, and then on to more important matters. Now it was time to send her on her way. If that was the case, she wanted to hear him say it—say she meant nothing to him and that he didn't want her the same way she wanted him.

She slipped between two sturdy beams that supported the topmost arch of the barn and then stopped to lean against a built-in ladder that led to the loft. She hooked the heel of her boot on the first rung.

It was show time.

Chapter Eleven

Darlene clung to the sides of the ladder, an unexpected surge of familiarity washing over her and leaving her dizzy and weak.

Climb the ladder. All the way to the top.

The words were spoken so clearly in her mind, she thought for a minute they had come from Clint. But no, he was still at the door with Randy. Pain thrummed in her fingertips. Looking down, she found her hands clenched so tightly around the wooden rails that her knuckles had turned white.

She closed her eyes, shuddering, suddenly overcome with emotion she didn't understand. When she opened her eyes, Clint was standing inches away. The last beam of the setting sun flickered through the windows above the loft, casting an almost eerie glow about his features. His face was a stony mask that revealed nothing, but his eyes betrayed him. Smoky with desire, they reached inside her and twisted around her heart.

Her breath caught in her throat, as wisps of memory rushed her mind. She'd been here before, in this very spot. With Clint. She knew it, as surely as she knew she'd just driven back from town with Randy. The details were shadowy silhouettes in a muddied pool, but the feeling was crystalline.

She reached out, and Clint took her hand. "Let's go back to the house," he urged. "It'll be dark soon."

"Not so dark. There's a full moon tonight." She tugged on his hand until he stepped closer. "Climb up in the loft with me, Clint."

He drew his lips into tight lines. "Why are you doing this, Darlene?"

"I have questions that need answers."

"We can talk better in the house." He nudged at the imposing Stetson, pushing it back farther on his head, so that he could look up at her.

She climbed another rung but didn't let go of his hand. The void stretched between them. "Did we make love in your barn, Clint?"

He exhaled slowly, audibly, and she sensed more than saw the agony that bunched his muscles and clenched his jaw. He let go of her hand and backed away.

"Don't go there, Darlene. Not tonight. Not now."

"I have to. I can't leave with so many things unsettled between us. Don't you see? You have the memories. All I have is whispers of what we were like together. Echoes of what it was like when we made love."

"You're lucky."

"Lucky that I don't remember how good it was, or that I don't know how wrong we were together?"

"Let it go."

He was pleading. But so was she. If she let it go now, they might never reach this point again—not if she was leaving tomorrow. Releasing his hand, she scurried up a few more rungs. "What were we, Clint?" She tossed the taunt over her shoulder. "Too good to give it another try, or so bad you can't bear to touch me again?"

He leaned into the ladder. "Did you remember something today? Is that what this is about?"

"I remember something now." Her words stuck in her throat, coming out a hoarse whisper.

"What is it you remember, Darlene?"

"A feeling. An ache." She trembled, and her voice broke at the admission. "I remember being in this loft with my pulse racing so fast I thought I might die with wanting you."

The ladder shook as Clint climbed aboard. She raced to the top and still beat him by only a few heart-stopping seconds. She rolled away from the opening, straw scattering under her, sticking to her hair and crawling into her boots.

Clint slid into the hay beside her, propped on one elbow, his face mere inches from hers. His fingers walked the flesh of her arm, climbed to her shoulder and then outlined her lips in warm, circular, sensual movements.

"I'll tell you what loving you was like."

She could all but hear the pain inside him as the words escaped his mouth. That was how husky, how desperate they sounded in the quiet of the moment.

"Loving you was like being ten years old and riding the fastest horse, leaving all the others far behind. Like riding the Ferris wheel at the county fair by yourself for the very first time and getting stopped at the top." His breath was hot on her flesh, his lips touching the lobe of her ear as he whispered. "Loving you was like fireworks on the Fourth of July, exploding into a million dazzling colors."

He stopped talking and his fingers stilled. She sensed a chill between them as he pulled away ever so slightly and directed his next words to the rough planks of the ceiling. "Fireworks that exploded brilliantly and then dissolved into nothing more than smoke on a restless wind."

"Why, Clint? What made it dissolve? What split us up?"

He tossed his hat and rolled to lie flat on his back, dropping his head to the pillow of hay. "The magic died."

"I don't believe that." This time she rolled on her side, pressing her body into his. "If the magic had died, you wouldn't be here lying beside me now. I wouldn't be burning inside with wanting you. You wouldn't be fighting so hard not to let me know that you want me the same way."

"Is that what you think, Darlene, that I can't get the taste of you off my lips, can't get the thrill of you out of my soul?"

"Yes."

The word was no more than a movement of her lips, a mingling of breaths as she touched her mouth to his. By choice, she stole away his chance to argue, robbed him of time to convince his body to lie the way his lips had done.

He shuddered beneath her as the kiss deepened, groaned in bittersweet agony as his arms wrapped around her, and his hands splayed across her back.

The kiss swam through her senses, filling her body with a yearning so intense that she struggled for breath. But still, she couldn't pull away—not with her body pressing into his, her heart beating against his chest, his hard need for her thrusting against the stiff fabric of his jeans.

Finally, struggling for breath, he rolled her off him and settled her on her side. His fingers tore clumsily at the buttons on her shirt. She didn't help him, didn't want to rush one second. She had to grab what she could, savor all the precious moments of anticipation. She ran a finger down his abdomen and then tugged his own shirt from his waistband.

When the last button was finally released, Clint tore her shirt loose, pushing it back from her shoulders and burying his face in the heated swell of her breasts. She trembled as his tongue circled nipples already peaked to an erotic high. His fingers seared her flesh, working their way around her to loose the hook that held her bra.

Each movement, each touch, brought new waves of pleasure. Shifting, she began to undress him, needing to feel as well as see his bare, ruggedly bronzed chest against the soft, untanned flesh of her breasts.

"Did I always need you so desperately?" she whispered, as her hands reached beneath his shirt and frolicked in the curl of dark hairs.

"Never as much as I needed you. Though I never stopped hoping that you would."

"I do now, Clint. I want you so badly, I feel the throbbing clear through to my soul."

"For now you do." He rocked her to him, his lips on her mouth and then her neck, tracing a fiery path that seared to the very core of her longing. "But I can't fight it any longer. I'll take *now*."

The words were like a reprieve, releasing the last remnants of his restraint, freeing him to make love to her the way she wanted it. Unbridled. Free and wild as the Texas wind.

He tore the clothes from her body in quick bursts of energy, punctuating each success with kisses and moans of pleasure. She wanted the thrill to last forever, but knew they would both die of unfulfilled passion if he didn't move to possess her all the way—and soon.

"I can't wait any longer, Darlene. I'm bursting with the need of you."

"I know. I'm ready. I think I always have been."

He lifted himself over her, his naked, muscular body gleaming in the incandescent shivers of the last light of day. She guided him into her, quivering as he entered. The anticipation had been exquisite. But the thrill of melting with him, her heart racing, her insides dissolving into liquid fire, was pure ecstasy. She cried out in pleasure, and then exploded with him as he thrust quickly before driving their passion home.

Minutes later, still warm and glowing, she felt the wetness of a tear on her check. She wiped it away with the back of her hand.

Clint pulled away enough to see her face. "Did I hurt you?"

"Oh, no. It's nothing like that."

"You're not sorry, are you?"

She trembled at the disappointment that came through in his voice. "I'm only sorry about one thing."

His body tensed, and she hurried to ease his concern. "I'm sorry for losing even one second of the memory of loving you before." She buried her head in his chest.

"Don't be," he whispered, holding her to him as though he would never let her go. "It was never more perfect than this."

For once, she believed him completely. She knew, even though she had no idea where or how she knew the truth of it, that this had been more than two people finding satisfaction in the act of making love.

This was love.

But the afterglow of passion would fade all too soon. Probably one second after she informed Clint that she would not be boarding a plane bound for Washington, D.C., in the morning.

JAMES MARSHALL McCORD SAT in the dank motel, his hand circling a glass of bourbon. He reached to massage the pain in his leg, drawing back his hand when he remembered that the leg was no longer there. It didn't bother him much anymore, though it had crushed him when he'd woken up and found it gone.

But even then, he'd never been sorry about the action that had cost him the leg. Loss was part of living. The same way loving was. The same way work and responsibility were. A man did what he had to do, and the truth was that he'd never been sorry for much of anything he'd done, as long as his heart was in the right place.

A man had to live with himself, first; his family, second; his neighbors, third. From the dusty trails of Vaquero, Texas, to the wide, plush halls of the White House. It all boiled down to the fundamentals of life. A real man did what he had to do when he had to do it.

Whether or not he could do it was the measure of a man—his totality. In war and peace. And in love.

He sipped the whiskey straight—the way he liked it best—so he could enjoy the burn as the amber liquid slid down his throat.

He wasn't sorry, but he did have regrets. The biggest one right now was that he'd been forced to pull the trigger on a day so long ago it should be cloaked in obscurity, veiled by time and distance. Instead, the day was as vivid in his mind's eye as if it had been yesterday. As if that jungle of war he'd endured was still going on around him. So vivid he could still feel the warmth from the flames as the encampment went up in smoke.

Now he'd drawn Darlene into his own personal nightmare as well. He'd rattled the skeletons of his past in her face, and then left her alone to face a madman who had nurtured his hatred for decades, who had held on to it until the need for revenge had eaten away at his brain and left him no more than an insane assassin.

A man does what he has to do.

The words took on the power of a mantra, echoing in McCord's head. He'd do what he had to do one more time, but he had to work fast: find the man responsible for trying to kill him and Darlene before the man found her.

The brother of the man he'd killed in Vietnam would find Darlene eventually, McCord knew, unless he stopped him first. He'd kill Darlene—and Clint too, if he got in the way.

"Clint." The name lingered on his tongue. Caulder said he'd underestimated the man. Maybe he had, but he could never see the man Clint had grown into without seeing the boy he used to be. Sitting in church between his parents. His mother looking soft and sweet, more like an angel than a mortal. Clint looking so much like the man who'd sired him that it hurt to look at him.

McCord's shoulders sagged from fatigue and the weight of his thoughts as he sipped the last of the whiskey. Clint had turned out like his old man in a lot of ways. Too quick to temper, too hardheaded, too proud to chase after the woman he loved. But he was young. He still had lots of time to learn, lots of time to experience life.

That wasn't true for McCord. He'd tasted everything life had to offer. That's why he had to make sure it was he, and not Clint, who dealt with Jake Edwards. Jake, just like his brother, would insist that it be a battle to the death.

Not that McCord was tired of living. Hell, no! He was graying and maybe slowing down a step every now and then, but he was as exhilarated over the future as ever. Ready to climb on the back of the millennium bull and ride it to the ground. Ready to pack up his boots and saddle and take up residence in the White House if the country wanted his leadership.

But first he had one more bit of dirty business to take care of. With good luck, it would soon be over. With bad luck...

He got up from the chair, walked to the window and stared out into the night. He couldn't let himself think of failure. Push had come to shove. He'd do what he had to do.

Chapter Twelve

Clint stretched awake as a mockingbird outside his window launched into a daybreak concert. His limbs ached, blessedly so, from a night of making love, but his body reveled in the comfort of his own bed. He'd all but forgotten how soft a mattress could be after almost a week on his lumpy couch. Giving in to a yawn, he reached for Darlene.

His insides coiled in anticipation at the prospect of taking her in his arms again and cuddling her naked body against his. He burrowed his hand under the covers and came up with a fistful of pillow.

He looked over and found what he'd feared. Darlene was no longer beside him. Apprehension did the job usually provided by the first cup of strong coffee; in fact, he shrugged off the dregs of sleep in record time. Swinging his bare legs over the side of the bed, he hit the floor on the run, slowing only long enough to grab his briefs from the floor and wiggle into them.

The aromas of freshly brewed coffee and frying bacon wafted down the hall from the kitchen. He breathed more easily, and slowed his step. She'd just gotten up before him for a change and was already cooking breakfast. Probably needed to finish packing for her flight home.

The thought of her leaving hit his already sore and achy body with a wallop to the gut. He sucked it up and kept walking. Last night was every bit as wonderful as he'd dreamed it would be—and a million times worse than he'd feared.

If anything at all had changed in the way he felt about her, it was that he loved her even more now than he had six years ago, meaning the parting would be pure hell. But at least this time when they said goodbye, they would both be hurting.

She fancied herself in love with him. Strangely enough, she was convinced that she'd always been. She'd find out differently once her memory returned. Everything new would be old again, and the cowboy who'd saved her life would be just good ol' Clint Richards from Vaquero, Texas.

The FBI would welcome her back with open arms, and this week would be history. The same way he'd be history....

He halted at the kitchen door and stared at the empty coffee cup and the note she'd left beside it. His bare feet slapped against the cold tile as he went to retrieve it. It was too soon for a Dear John. Bernie wouldn't show up to drive her to the airport for another hour. He picked up the paper and held it up to catch the early light creeping through the window.

Last night was wonderful. This morning is splendid. I've gone for a ride on Brandy. Catch me if you can. Clue: I packed a picnic breakfast to eat at the top of the hill beyond the corral. Meet me under the tallest pine. But first call Bernie and tell him to save himself a trip in to San Antonio. I've already canceled my reservation on the flight.

Clint wadded the paper and tossed it, giving it a kick for good measure when he passed it on his way to the bedroom for a pair of jeans. And to think some men just woke up on Sunday morning to a nice cup of hot coffee and the funny papers.

CLINT STOPPED on a narrow ridge. The land to the east of him was mostly open pasture. To the west was a hilly wooded area that stretched for half a mile, winding upward to the top of Piney Knoll and then rolling downward to the creek bed. If he'd been forced to search for Darlene without directions it might have taken him hours, but she'd been specific.

She'd better be where she'd said. He was in no mood for this kind of game, not with a killer on the loose. It was unthinkable that she'd gone off by herself like this, but he wasn't surprised. Her personality hadn't changed just because she didn't remember the past.

She had never been the kind of woman to take orders, especially his. But this morning's action was dangerous, and he wouldn't put up with any more such shenanigans. Like it or not, if she stayed in Vaquero, she was under his protection. Even sleeping with the lawman on duty didn't change that.

He led his horse up the rocky incline, talking her through the trail. This wasn't the easiest of rides, but Darlene was an experienced horsewoman. They'd traveled this path countless times the summer…

His mind hedged, the way it always did when it came to defining that summer and what had made it so different from any other of his life. The summer he and Darlene had made love. The summer she'd burrowed under his skin and into his heart, carved out her own niche so perfectly that he'd never be able to fit anyone else into it.

The summer his mother had died. The summer he'd learned things about himself that he'd never wanted to know. The summer he found out what it cost to lose the woman he loved.

The footing grew less slippery, and he urged his horse to a trot. The worrisome unease that had hounded him ever since he'd found Darlene's note intensified. He grabbed a deep breath and grappled with his fears.

The truth was, Darlene was probably safe enough out here, especially since he'd had Dr. Bennigan spread the lies about her. The doctor was to tell anyone who asked that Darlene had suffered significant brain damage and that her memory wouldn't return. The rumor would have reached half the town by now. Vaquero might be behind the times in most areas, but its rumor mill was state-of-the-art.

Darlene would be furious if she found out, but he hadn't planned on her being around after today to find out. It was the killer he wanted to convince. If Clint could buy some time, he could figure it all out, determine who it was that had been threatening McCord and why. He could put the man behind bars even without McCord's help.

He stretched high in the saddle as he reached the top of the grassy knoll, scanning the area quickly. Darlene was probably nearby, enjoying an early morning ride on the back of a magnificent animal. Still, he'd breathe easier once he spotted her.

He heard her first. She was singing, something current from the radio, though he couldn't have given it a name if his life depended on it. His fears subsided, but his heart rate doubled. On their first date, she'd sung along with the radio. Knew every word to every song, even the moldy oldies.

He'd loved it—not that her voice was anything special, but her enthusiasm was infectious. It was hard to be down or to take yourself too seriously when she was belting out an old Beatles tune. He walked his horse toward her, drinking in the sight.

There was nothing fancy about her. But he loved the way her straight, silky hair blew in the wind. Loved the gentle sway of her hips when she walked. Grew painfully hard at the sight of her cute little bottom in the tight jeans.

He pulled his hat lower on his head, blocking the first serious rays of morning sun, and chastised himself for entertaining such destructive thoughts. Fool that he was, he liked everything about her. Just as he had six years ago.

Taking the reins firmly in hand the way he should have done his heart, he rode fast and hard to the top of the hill.

"HOWDY, MA'AM. This is private property, you know, and you're trespassing."

Darlene smiled at the sound of the exaggerated Texas drawl, relieved that it wasn't booming anger. "It's okay. I sleep with the owner."

Clint climbed down from the horse he was riding and tied him next to Brandy. "I don't think the owner got a lot of sleep last night."

She finished spreading the plaid tablecloth on the ground before she walked over and slipped her arms about his waist. "Are you complaining?"

He reached under her jacket to pull her close. Her lips were puckered and waiting, but the cold metal at his fingertips made him pull away as if he'd been bitten by a rattlesnake.

"Since when did you start wearing a gun?"

"I don't know. I guess since I joined up with the FBI. Evidently I'm not a 'desk' type."

Darlene cocked her head back to study his expression. His eyes had lost the gleam of desire and grown dark and stormy.

"You're on leave. Where did you get the gun?" His voice was frigid.

She held her ground. "I found it stashed away in one of my suitcases. Evidently I brought it with me, so I must know how to use it."

"So, with gun in hand, you take off on your own. Did you think that carrying a gun was going to put you on even footing with the killer? Did you think that you could just go canceling airline flights and disregarding my advice because you found a weapon in your luggage?"

She inhaled slowly, gathering her wits and her nerve to stand up against Clint's practiced intimidation techniques. She stiffened her backbone and held her head high. "Yes."

"Yes?" Now his voice was booming.

"Yes. But I didn't disregard your advice. I weighed it carefully. In the end, I decided that it was best for me to stay in Vaquero."

"I'd like to know how you came to that decision."

"And I'd like to tell you. After breakfast. Now, if you'll get that thermos out of my saddlebag and pour the coffee, I'll get the egg and bacon burritos. They're wrapped inside a towel with a hot tile, so they should still be warm."

The fire in his eyes dimmed a little. "We'll eat, but that doesn't mean this discussion is over."

"Of course not. But heated discussions are bad for digestion."

Clint poured the coffee, while Darlene filled the plastic plates with burritos, a smattering of salsa, and half a peeled orange. She settled on the edge of the cloth, Indian-style, and waited until Clint had done the same before lifting her cup of strong, black coffee in a toast.

"To making more new memories."

Clint clinked his cup with hers. "You might not want the new ones when the old ones return."

"A gorgeous and heroic cowboy, making breath-stealing love on a bed of hay, and a sunrise breakfast on a hilltop. What's not to want?"

"I don't know. When you remember, you tell me."

Clint's tone more than his words cut into the fabric of their morning. Earlier, while riding Brandy across acres of open spaces, she'd almost been able to forget the reason she was here. She'd almost been able to believe that she didn't need the lost memories, that who she was right now was enough.

But in truth, the forgotten past stood between her and the present as surely as the barbwire stood between Clint's cattle and his neighbor's pasture. Not only her personal relationships, but her very life was balanced on threads of memory that had retreated to dark crevices where her conscience couldn't find them.

They ate the rest of the meal in a strained silence. Darlene only nibbled at the last half of her burrito, but Clint ate every bite and then used an extra tortilla to scoop up the egg and bacon that had fallen onto his plate. His appetite was apparently not affected by his mood.

She waited until he finished, and then moved backward until she could extend her legs fully and use the stump of a tree trunk for a backrest. She'd already asked the question that clouded the air between them more than once, but this time she wasn't going to settle for less than the truth. Or at least, the truth as Clint had interpreted it.

"Why did we break up six years ago, Clint? What happened between us?"

"Nothing as dramatic as you seem to be looking for. You just changed your mind about wanting to be my wife."

"Had you asked me to?"

"I proposed."

"And I said yes. Had we planned the wedding?"

"No. My mother was terminally ill with cancer. We decided to wait so that I could devote my time to making her as comfortable as I could during the last painful weeks."

"Surely I didn't mind that?"

"No. You couldn't have been more understanding. Both of you cried when you showed her your engagement ring."

Clint talked slowly, as if he were reluctant to pull the facts out of their shadowed hiding places and expose them to the light. But she had to know. It was the only way she could make sure that page of history didn't repeat itself.

"Something had to happen to send me running away, Clint. I didn't wake up one day and decide I wanted out."

"What makes you so sure?"

"Last night." She swallowed and stumbled with the task of putting her feelings into words. "No one could walk away from what we shared last night."

"We made love last night, Darlene. It was exciting." He fingered the brim of his hat and stared into space for long seconds before locking his gaze with hers. "No, it was more than exciting. It was all a man could ever want from a woman. But it isn't life."

He was making excuses, either for her or himself. For all she knew those excuses had become fact to him, but she recognized them for what they were. Feeble, ego-saving excuses that relieved him of responsibility in whatever had happened between them.

"Why don't you tell me what life is in your book, Clint?"

He crossed his arms in front of him and tipped his hat back. "It's not *my* book. It's the way it is. Life as my wife would have meant waking up every morning to a day not much different from the one before. It would have meant having the same view outside your window, running into the same people in the same grocery store, eating the same meal at Rosita's when the urge to eat out hit you. You weren't ready for that."

She reached for the thermos and refilled their cups, this time sitting down on the edge of the cloth closest to him. "Were those my words?"

"No." He swatted at a mosquito that darted about his face, his muscles as strained as if he'd been attacking a wildcat. "Your words were that *McCord* had intervened, and that you had been admitted to the training program at Quantico after all. *McCord* thought you would make a wonderful agent and you decided to go for it. After all, *McCord* had been like a father to you, and you didn't want to disappoint *him*."

McCord. The name was poison on Clint's tongue. And, just as she'd expected, his distaste for McCord had colored their breakup, at least in his mind. And now McCord was playing another major role in their relationship—ironically enough, bringing them back together.

"Tell me about McCord, Clint. What did he do that turned you against him this way when everyone else in the free world sees him as just a little beneath the second coming?''

Clint stretched to his feet and picked up his dirty plate and cup, wiping them clean with the corner of his napkin. ''What did McCord do to me? Nothing. Absolutely nothing.''

She'd expected the comment to reek of bitterness. What she hadn't expected was the hurt that crept into his voice. Standing, she walked behind him and snaked her arms about his waist, burying her head against his strong back.

''When this is over, Clint, I won't be marching to McCord's orders. Whatever happens to us will be our doing. I just want you to know that.''

Clint turned and pulled her into his arms. She trembled, as always, at his touch. Tucking a thumb under her chin, he tilted her face upward and let his lips brush hers—a feather of a kiss that left her aching for more.

''I'll hold you to that,'' he whispered, his promise half swallowed by a gust of wind. ''Now, all we have to do is keep you alive. Which brings up the real issue of the day.'' He lifted her off the ground and sat her on the tree stump, bringing them eye to eye. ''If you ever go off on your own again before this killer is found, I'll lock you in that cold, dingy jail of mine and bury the key in a haystack.''

He was back in his element. The Texas sheriff at his best. Fighting the bad guys and protecting his citizenry. He oozed power. And masculinity.

She hushed his words with her lips, catching the breath of his anger and mingling it with her desire. This time, he didn't pull away until she'd been properly kissed.

''Kiss or no kiss, I meant what I said about your not going off half cocked and unprotected, Darlene.''

"Yes sir, Sheriff. Whatever you say."

She tipped her hat and jumped down from the stump. She knew Clint was anxious to get out to the Altamira and dig up anything that might give him a lead. She planned to go with him. She was up to her eyeballs in this mess, and she couldn't help but believe that if she could hit on the right fact, the events of Monday night would come toppling down on top of her.

And once those facts hit home, the rest of her memory would probably follow close behind, all tied to Mc-Cord—like a stick of dynamite, delivered and ready to blow.

It was clear Clint knew something about McCord that he wasn't willing to share, not even with her. But she might know far worse already. McCord might have told her something so horrifying that she closed her mind to everything, rather than face the truth about him.

She busied herself packing away the used dishes, while Clint scraped the remainder of her food out for the scavenging birds and animals and emptied the last drops of coffee from the thermos.

Her mind whirled dizzily with the events of the last few days, and she wondered how she'd ever handled a lifetime of problems. Still, one of her questions had been answered, and though the answer didn't make her feel a bit better about herself, she could live with it.

If Clint had read her past actions right, she'd broken her engagement with Clint because she'd been young and had craved adventure. Things were drastically different now. She wasn't so young anymore. And while she wasn't sure about the woman who'd lived in her body before last Monday night, she was sure about the one who lived here now. The current Darlene Remington was totally in love with Clint Richards.

DARLENE STEPPED OVER an open cardboard box stuffed to the brim with old letters, pictures, magazines and newspaper articles yellowed with age. She maneuvered the narrow maze among additional boxes and crawled back into the attic nest she'd made for herself from a Mexican blanket and a huge plastic beanbag chair.

"I'd hate to be around when McCord finds out the two of you have been rummaging through his attic and perusing his personal records."

Darlene looked up from the article she was skimming to appraise the silvery-blond man who had just poked his head through the attic opening. As usual, Thornton Roberts wore a smirk on his face that indicated he was just a shade above the Altamira family he was paid to protect, and way above the rest of Vaquero's residents.

Clint looked up from the letter he was reading. "I'm surprised to hear that, Thornton. I'd have guessed you'd be the first one to tell McCord, seeing as how you disapprove so heartily."

"I'm old-fashioned, Sheriff. I expect lawmen to obey the law."

"Then you'd be pleased to know I have permission to be here and to peruse these records."

"I'd like to know how you got that permission. McCord hasn't been heard from in days. I, for one, think the federal authorities should be alerted that he hasn't been seen since the attack on Monday night. Emory, of course, thinks we shouldn't do anything to provoke negative publicity."

"For once, I agree with him. What do you think the authorities would do if you called them?" Clint asked, folding the letter he'd been reading and stuffing it back in the yellowed envelope. "McCord called and said he was fine, that he wanted some time to himself. That's not a felony—not even for a future president.''

"He might have called under duress. For all we know, there might have been a gun poked in his rib cage while he talked.''

"And for what purpose? We haven't had any demands for ransom or political favors in exchange for his release.''

Thornton climbed the rest of the way into the attic. He squatted near Clint. "Tell me the truth, Sheriff. You're not as addle-brained as that personal bodyguard who's not guarding a body. Not as dense as Freddie Caulder either. What do you really make of this?''

"What do I make of what?''

"Of McCord's disappearance. I mean, the man walks out of here last Monday with Darlene, here, on his arm. He's smiling, talking to everybody, acting like everything is fine and dandy. The next we hear, he's been attacked. His blood is on Darlene's blouse, his wallet's recovered in the woods, and nobody's seen the man since. Yet, the only word I get is to keep extra men on duty around the clock, and if anyone suspicious comes around, don't let them out of sight.''

"Who'd you get that word from?''

"Freddie Caulder. That's the other thing that burns me. I'm the one hired to handle security around here, and yet Caulder's the only one McCord talks to when he calls.''

"McCord's a rancher. Caulder's his foreman. Not to mention that they've been friends for years. He's only known you, what…ten or twelve months?''

"I've been head of security here for six months. But just because I'm new around here doesn't mean I can't see what's going on under my own nose.''

The expression on Clint's face shifted from barely tolerant to highly interested. He leaned forward, planting his elbows on his thighs. "If you've got a point to make, Thornton, let's hear it."

"Okay. I don't have any proof, mind you, but I think Caulder was in on what happened Monday night."

"What makes you say that?"

"The way he's acting. He's nervous, jumps every time you walk up behind him. And who's to say he's really talked to McCord? The senator might be dead, for all we know. He's liable to be a buzzard buffet right now while we're talking about him."

The image rumbled through Darlene's mind, and twisted sickeningly in her stomach. "I talked to McCord," she said when the wave of nausea passed.

"You talked to someone who said he was McCord. You have no way of knowing who it really was, since you can't remember him. Don't you think it strange that no one else has talked to him? Not even Mary, and she's been friends every bit as long as Caulder. She practically raised his daughter, if you can believe what she says."

"If Mary says it, it's true," Clint put in.

Thornton pulled a handkerchief from his pocket. He dabbed at his forehead and the back of his neck. "I don't know how you people stand the heat up here, or why you'd want to spend hours in a musty attic. The evidence you need is outside, riding around on one of McCord's horses."

Darlene considered his statement while he backed out of the attic. She could hear the *clomp* of his footsteps on the ladder and feel the vibration when he jumped from the last rung to the carpeted floor of the hall.

"Want to take a break?" Clint asked, dropping the stack of letters from his lap and coming over to sit beside her.

"Not unless you do. These letters are fascinating, but I'm doubtful I'll find anything useful in them. McCord just talks about the beauty of the countryside and tells stories of the men who were in his unit."

"I'm sure he didn't want to worry his mother any more than she was already. The horrors of the Vietnam war were on the nightly news in living color."

"Are we breaking the law reading these without McCord's permission?"

"We would be if they were his."

"Who do they belong to? They're addressed to his mother, but she's dead."

"They belong to McCord's daughter, Levi, now. Her grandmother split her personal effects between Levi and her cousin Robin, but they never separated the memoirs. Levi faxed me permission to look through the records yesterday. She worries for her father. I think if it were up to her, he'd get out of politics altogether and run the ranch."

"It must be difficult doing both, especially now, with all the hype about the millennium stirring up the loonies. Did you ever think of going into politics, Clint?"

"For about five minutes, one time. A committee came to my house requesting that I run for mayor."

"What made you decide to turn them down?"

"I used the balance method. Cattle on one side, people on the other. The cattle won, hands down."

"But you like being sheriff?"

He linked his hands behind his neck and leaned back, stretching. "I like parts of it. Other parts I tolerate. I like the challenge of stopping some people from running over others. I like taking brutal, vicious people off the street so decent people don't have to fear them. I don't like losing—and that's what I feel is happening now. That's why I won't rest until I find the man who tried to kill you."

"Maybe he's given up, decided I'm not worth the effort."

Clint reached over and took both her hands in his. "Don't think that for a second, Darlene. If you think that way, you'll let your guard down. That's what he's waiting on. That split-second window of opportunity when he can strike and not be caught."

"Then why did he leave the other night when he was waiting outside Bledsoe's gate?"

"Because he's smart and cautious. This is not a crime of passion but of design. He plans to kill, and get away with it. If he had shot one or both of us the other night after Leon spotted him, he would have been the prime suspect in the murders. So he left, decided to bide his time. But he won't wait forever."

Gooseflesh popped out on her arms, and she felt the chill deep inside. "You're frightening me, Clint."

He slid a hand to the back of her head, tangling his fingers in her hair. "Good. A healthy fear will help keep you alive. That, and a good sheriff on your arm."

He touched his lips to hers, and she melted into him. The kiss was long and wet and sweet. "I do like your protection policy," she said when he finally pulled away. "But I think we better continue this part of it later in the privacy of your home."

"Or my barn."

This time she kissed him.

It was long minutes later when she settled back into the letters. And another hour before she finally noticed a pattern that piqued her interest. She reread one particular letter, excitement building with every word.

"Can you come over here a minute, Clint? I think I may have hit on something here."

Chapter Thirteen

Clint left the antique metal trunk he'd been perched on and peered over Darlene's shoulder. "Let's see what you've got."

She handed him a yellowed letter, some of the words smudged from humidity and time. "Read the date on that letter."

He did. Nothing unusual registered with him. The letter opened with the young Jim McCord saying he was sorry for the time lapse since the last letter. He'd been busy. Clint skimmed the remaining three paragraphs quickly, and then a second time since he found nothing to trigger any excitement.

"He wrote this four months before he lost his leg. He talks about the weather and asks about the local high-school basketball game. That's all I see. Am I missing something?"

She waved a stack of letters she had clasped in her hand. "McCord wrote his mother faithfully every Wednesday for a year. Long, detailed letters that described the country, the men in his unit, the camaraderie that was developing among them. Every positive thing he could think of. The letters are so engrossing, they'd make a wonderful book."

"So, he was a dutiful son. How does that fit in with what we're looking for?"

"There was a span of seven weeks between the last letter and the one I showed you. Seven weeks when he apparently had no contact with his mother."

"He wrote that he was busy. Did you find something that would indicate otherwise?"

"A pattern that developed—a mood swing that seemed to evolve around a man he referred to as Whacko."

Clint settled on the blanket beside Darlene, a stir of anticipation sweetening the stale attic air. "Show me what you mean by 'mood swing.'"

"For nearly a year, the letters were only upbeat, but slowly a touch of negativism crept in. Most of the time his goal in writing seemed to be to reassure his mother, but just before the time lapse, it seemed he was the one who needed reassuring."

"The perils of war. He was probably seeing more dangerous action."

"No. At first I thought that. But I read the letters again, and the concern seems to be about the soldier he called Whacko. He asks his mother what would make a man lash out at the people who looked to him for support. And in this one letter…" She shuffled through a sheaf of letters and pulled one from the stack as if she were drawing from an Old Maid hand. Dropping the others to her lap, she carefully slipped another letter from a torn envelope. "This one made me shudder." She read the letter out loud.

"I can hear the fire from a nearby battle as I write this letter. Men are dying. Yet even while I sit here thinking how fortunate I am to be alive, part of me feels guilty. Why was their life stolen from them and mine spared?

"If I return from the war in good health, I will owe something back to the God who sees me through this. I will no longer be content to live peacefully on my ranch without any thought for the millions of people who are less fortunate than we have always been."

A choking knot swelled in Clint's throat as he listened to Darlene. This was a side of McCord he didn't know. The man when he'd been even younger than Clint was now. The age he'd been right before Clint's mother had first met him, a wounded soldier coming home from the war.

Darlene cleared her throat, smoothed the wrinkles from the page.

"But death is not what troubles me the most. I fear most what friends do to friends. Not all friends, of course, but one man in particular who turns on his friends for no apparent reason. The name Whacko was given in jest when we first met him, but it was more apt than we'd ever dreamed. The man has gone over the edge, and still we are forced to follow his command or risk a court martial."

The rest of the letter was an apology for sharing his dark thoughts with his mother. He assured her he'd be fine and that he'd write as soon as the A-Team he'd been assigned to returned from an upcoming mission.

"What do you think, Clint? Could this be the link we're looking for? It's far-fetched, I know, but do you think this Whacko could be the man who's threatening

McCord now? The man who attacked me on Glenn Road and tried to kill me in the hospital?''

Clint exhaled—a long, slow, exasperated release—and stretched to his feet. He thought best standing, or, more often, pacing. The cramped attic offered little opportunity for that, but he paraded the small square of open space, his mind wrestling with possibilities.

''Thirty years is a long time to carry a grudge,'' he said, more talking things through to himself than making conversation. ''But I guess it's possible. If something happened between the two of them while they were on that mission. Something that stuck in Whacko's craw and agitated him over the years. Or if McCord's recent notoriety has angered him, reawakened the bitter feelings and made him determined to put an end to McCord's bid for the presidency. But what could McCord have done to him to make—''

Darlene sucked in a ragged breath. Her face had turned in seconds from healthy pink to a ghastly white.

Clint knelt and took her hand. ''What's wrong?''

''The hallucination. The soldiers. The jungle. The murder. Could McCord have killed one of Whacko's friends? Or perhaps he killed *Whacko,* and one of his buddies has come back to exact revenge?''

She collapsed against him, her heart beating so hard that he could feel it through their clothes. He stroked her hair, wanting to comfort her and not having the slightest idea how. Not when what she feared smoldered in his own mind as well. Had James McCord been a party to murder? And if he had killed someone, had he followed Whacko's orders or had the deed been his own?

''There's no use speculating, Darlene. There are records on battles, on who was killed on what dates, on which men were assigned to specific units. It'll take some digging, but it's not impossible to find.''

"Something happened on that mission, Clint. I know it did. Something that changed McCord's life. He didn't write his mother for seven weeks after that, and when he did finally write, the letters were short and impersonal, almost as if he were writing them to a stranger.''

"Something happened. Now we have to find out what. And hope this incident is related to the problems we're having in Vaquero.''

"No matter what I saw in the hallucination, I can't believe McCord is a murderer. I *won't* believe it.''

"Such loyalty toward a man you don't even remember.'' Clint massaged her shoulders and the back of her neck. He could feel the tightness of the muscles and imagine the strain she was going through.

"He was my friend. Surely I have better judgment than that. And millions of Americans trust him.'' She put her hands on top of his as he massaged. "What about you, Clint? Do you believe he could have committed murder?''

He struggled with his answer. Not to protect Darlene; she didn't need or expect to be protected from the truth. He wasn't so sure about himself. "I don't know, Darlene. I just don't know.''

She leaned into his hand, trapping it between her cheek and her shoulder. "Then that's your answer. I hope it's not based on the fact that he helped me get a position at Quantico. That wouldn't be fair to him or to me, and is certainly not pertinent to this issue.''

He pulled away at the sound of feet climbing the ladder outside the attic opening.

"Are you two going to stay up here all day? I can't

wait dinner much longer,'' Mary called, sticking her head with its tightly coiffed gray hair through the opening.

''You didn't need to cook for us,'' Darlene answered, her voice steady and solid again.

''Speak for yourself,'' Clint said, grabbing his hat. ''I'm famished, and Mary's the best cook north of the Rio Grande.'' He shoved a box out of Darlene's path with the toe of his boot. He was ready for food and action. It set better with him than dealing with McCord's emotional trappings from the past, and a whole lot better than dealing with his own feelings about a man he'd lost faith in years ago.

In spite of everything, he'd never wanted to believe in any man's innocence more than he wanted to believe in James McCord's.

DINNER WAS TO BE SERVED on a glassed-in porch that jutted off from the huge kitchen. Mary headed Darlene in that direction, refusing any help with putting the finishing touches on the meal. The table was set for six, but so far Darlene was the only one present besides the busy cook. Clint had washed his hands and then excused himself to use the phone.

The outside temperature hovered in the fifties, but the sunshine beaming through the window warmed the room so much that Darlene shrugged out of her sweater. Staring through the glass, she absorbed the quiet pastoral scene, and hoped it would still the dark thoughts that were running rampant through her mind.

Grasses, yellowed from a taste of early frost, carpeted the rolling hills. Beyond the pasture and the last row of barbwire, a border of green cedar and maples with a remaining smattering of gold and yellow leaves faded into the russet hues of bald rock.

She turned as Mary entered the door carrying a platter overflowing with fried chicken. "May I help you with that?"

"Not with this," she said, plopping it down in the dead center of the large round table. She stopped to smooth a wrinkle in the red-plaid cloth. "But I've got plenty more in the kitchen that needs totin' in here. I'd appreciate the help."

Darlene followed Mary back into the kitchen.

"If you can handle the mashed potatoes and gravy, I can get the rest."

"You mean there's more?"

"Not much. The biscuits are browning, and I've got winter turnip greens I just picked this morning. Then there's the banana pudding for dessert."

"You must have been cooking since daybreak."

"It didn't take me any time to put this little meal together. Nothing fancy—not like I try to do when the senator's here. Not that he complains about anything, but he's here so seldom, I try to cook his favorites."

Mary peeked inside the oven and wiped her hands on her apron. A habit, Darlene decided, since her hands were clean and dry.

"I'm so thankful Clint's here, doing what he can to help the senator," Mary said, fingering a row of eyelet trim on her apron. "Mr. McCord's a proud man, and he doesn't like to ask for help, but he knows what a good lawman Clint is. When Clint used to come over with Levi and her friends—you know, church socials and such— I'd catch Mr. McCord watching him. 'He's a fine young man, that Clint Richards.' That's what he used to say. If he said it once, he said it a dozen times."

"But he told Freddie Caulder he didn't want Clint involved in this."

"Well, like I said, he hates to admit he can't handle his own problems. He was quick enough to hire Thornton Roberts to oversee security at the ranch when the media started busting in here and those millennium end-of-the-worlders started putting up pickets. But you should have heard him howl when Whitt Emory told him he was hiring a bodyguard for him and that he was to take Bernie with him every time he left the ranch."

"It looks like Mr. Emory won the argument."

"He didn't, but he should have. If the senator had taken Bernie along with the two of you last week, you might not have gotten your head bashed in. You don't know how sad I was to hear you'd lost your memory for good."

"Where did you hear that?"

Mary's face flushed beet red. She grabbed a pot holder and rescued her biscuits from the oven. "I'm not spreading gossip, Darlene," she said, finally turning back to face her. "I was told it's common knowledge."

"You were told by whom?"

"Well, I head it from Susan Peters, and she heard it from Sally at the coffee shop, but she swore she got it firsthand from one of the nurses at the hospital." Mary stacked the hot biscuits on a plate, her fingers flying so fast that they didn't suffer from the heat. Not until she was finished did she turn to lock gazes with Darlene. "It is true, isn't it?"

"If it is, no one told me about it." Darlene tamped down the aggravation rumbling inside her. Mary meant well. It was senseless to take her anger out on the messenger. She'd save it until she found out who'd started the rumor, and why.

They were spared further conversation on the touchy

subject by the arrival of Bernie and Thornton, with Clint a few steps behind them.

"Did someone tell Caulder dinner was ready?" Bernie asked, forking a chicken breast and passing the plate on.

Mary stopped pouring tea into the ice-filled glasses. "I beeped him. He said he'd fix himself a plate later, when everyone was through."

"Humph. Guess he thinks he's too good to eat with us. I notice he ran in here fast enough yesterday when that guy Bledsoe showed up."

Clint sat the bowl of potatoes back on the table with a noisy clump. "What was Bledsoe doing out here?"

"You'd have to ask Caulder about that," Thornton said. "Some big secret between the three of them."

"The three of them?"

"Bledsoe, Caulder and McCord." This time it was Bernie supplying the information. "I'm on the payroll for the specific purpose of protecting McCord, yet he gets hurt and runs off to lick his wounds and plan his payback with his two old army buddies."

Clint put down his fork. "I didn't know they were all in the army together."

"That's what Thornton told me," Bernie said.

"I don't know it for a fact myself," Thornton cut in, "but I overheard Bledsoe and Caulder talking yesterday when they were trying to be so secretive. They were whispering about some photographs taken in Vietnam. I just took it to mean they'd been stationed together."

"How did you hear them if they were whispering?" Darlene asked, trying to make sense of the conversation.

Thornton smiled. "I don't give away my trade secrets, Miss Darlene, especially to FBI agents."

The conversation veered off to FBI policies and a half-dozen other topics. Darlene listened with half her mind, while the other half tangled with the day's discoveries and the continuing saga of how she'd gotten dragged into McCord's mess.

When the meal was over, she helped Mary clean up the kitchen, while the men talked in the other room. Ordinarily she would have loved listening to Mary's stories about the Altamira and the senator. Today, it was the men's talk she longed to hear.

DARLENE SAT on the top step of the ranch foreman's front porch, watching a couple of sassy squirrels playing chase at the foot of a pecan tree. Caulder stood, his back pressed against the wooden column that supported the roof. Clint had made a seat of the porch rail. They each nursed a cup of coffee that had sat in the pot until it screwed your mouth into puckered circles when you tried to drink it.

The appearance was of friends chatting on an early winter afternoon—unless you looked too closely at the faces of the men in question or picked up on the tension that shortened their sentences into darting questions and accusations.

"I promised McCord that Darlene would be on a flight back to the capital this morning," Caulder snapped, staring at her as if she were the troublemaker in all of this. "You made a liar out of me."

"I'll take responsibility for Darlene."

"No, I take responsibility for the decision not to leave," she said. "I'm an adult, not a child to be ordered around."

"Neither of you know what you're getting into," Caulder said.

"We're not 'getting' into it. We're already *in* it.

McCord took care of that when he invited Darlene down here and introduced her to a killer.''

"All the same, I'm warning you, Clint. You can't stop this man. I'm not even sure McCord can.''

"Then why doesn't McCord ask for help?''

"Because it's his fight. He didn't start it, but he's the one who'll have to end it.''

"No, Caulder.'' Clint slid from the porch rail and stepped closer to the foreman. "You know better. You're just parroting what McCord told you to say. And this isn't a deep, dark secret anymore. I know what happened in Vietnam.''

Darlene knew Clint was bluffing, but apparently it worked. Caulder turned to her. "You remembered, didn't you? I knew that story about your memory being lost for good couldn't be true.''

"She didn't remember anything, Caulder. We just dug through some boring war records. We know all about Whacko. Now, I want to know how to get in touch with McCord.''

"I don't know.'' His eyes darted from left to right, as if he expected to find someone sneaking up on them, listening to their conversation. "If you know what's going on, you know more than I do, Sheriff. McCord won't tell me nothing. He says this is nobody's business but his.''

Clint wrapped a fist around the collar of Caulder's shirt. "Don't make me arrest you as an unfriendly witness. Tell me where I can find McCord.''

"I don't know where he is. I swear. He calls me at night just to make sure everything's all right. That's all I know.''

"What did Bledsoe want?''

Caulder swallowed, his Adam's apple bobbing like

crazy. ''Pictures. Just some old pictures from McCord's army days and a notebook with phone numbers and addresses in it—stuff like that.''

Clint let go of Caulder's collar, but he didn't back off. ''Where did Bledsoe find the pictures McCord wanted?''

''In the top of Bledsoe's closet. We brought them out here so that we could go through them. The box is in the living room. You can look at them, if you want.''

''You're being awfully agreeable all of a sudden. I guess you're not too eager to visit my little jail.''

''It's not jail I'm afraid of. It's that cemetery out there. I don't know what McCord's up against, but it's more than just some harmless kook like he thought at first. He's scared too. I can hear it in his voice. Maybe not for himself, but for Darlene and for you, Clint, and even me. He wants all of us to stay clear of this.''

''It's a little late for that, Caulder. The trouble's boot high and getting deeper. Now, let me see what's left in the treasure chest.''

Darlene went through the boxes with Clint, while Caulder downed two beer and paced a nerve-racking trail from the fireplace to the door and back again. There were no photos of anyone named Whacko, or, if there were, that name wasn't written under the picture.

She gave up before Clint did. Bledsoe probably knew what he was looking for, but they were just stabbing in the dark. None of the men except McCord looked even vaguely familiar, and that was only because she'd seen his pictures on the walls of the Altamira. That didn't necessarily mean a thing. Men changed a lot from twenty to fifty—aged from pimples to wrinkles, from long thick hair to balding gray.

Clint walked over and stood in front of Caulder. ''I don't see you in any of these pictures.''

"And you won't. I wasn't in 'Nam."

Darlene rummaged to the bottom of the smaller box, where her fingers slid against the sharp edge of a picture frame. She pulled it out, brushing away the loose snapshots that littered the top, and stared at the photo.

She didn't recognize the woman, but she knew the man right away. It was McCord, though he looked different out of uniform. He was wearing a western shirt, his face much thinner than it had looked in the other photos. Her gaze fell to the left leg. There was no prosthesis, though she knew he had one now. Just the edge of his pants leg pinned up. A wooden crutch was propped under his armpit.

It wasn't the injury that touched her heart, but the way the man and the woman were looking at each other. If you could picture Love, this had to be it.

"This must have been taken a short time after McCord lost his leg."

Clint reached for the picture. She watched the muscles in his face clench as he stared at the photograph for several long moments before tossing it back into the box.

"The woman he was with was very pretty. Is that Levi's mother?"

"I don't know who the woman is."

"Sure you do, Clint." Caulder reached down and retrieved the picture, sitting it upright on the corner of the coffee table. "That's your momma before you were born."

The awkward silence that followed was excruciatingly long. Darlene made the first move to end it, saying she was tired and that she thought they'd looked through enough pictures.

She'd forgotten her past, but being involved with this investigation was forcing Clint to deal with his on a daily basis. She didn't know what role his mother had played in his problems with McCord, but it was evident in that picture that at one time the two of them had been very much in love. A fact that obviously did not set well with her son, even thirty years later.

Suddenly, Darlene longed to be alone with Clint, to nestle in his arms, to pretend for a few hours that everything was right with their world and that the only worry they had was whether they should make love in the hayloft or in the bed.

But the look on his face told her that wasn't going to happen tonight.

"I want McCord to call me, Caulder. Get him that message, and tell him I mean business."

"I can't tell him unless he calls me. I have no way of getting in touch with him."

"Just get him my message. And if you know anything at all about the man who's after McCord and Darlene, Caulder, tell me now." His muscles were coiled, his hands curled into tight fists. "If you don't, and I find out later that you could have, you'll wish your mom had been childless."

"If I knew anything I'd tell you, Clint." Caulder bit his bottom lip. "All I know is that McCord is fighting the first demon he might not be able to whip. And I know you better work fast. If you don't, it will be too late. For him and for Darlene. I just hope she didn't make a big mistake when she missed that plane this morning."

"You can relax. She'll be on the first one out in the morning." He shot her a look that dared her to argue.

She turned and walked outside without waiting for him. They'd discuss her leaving when they were back at his ranch house, and they'd discuss a couple of other issues as well. He claimed she left six years ago because she wanted a career and a life outside Vaquero. More likely, she thought now, she'd just wanted to share his.

Chapter Fourteen

Darkness fell early beneath a blanket of rolling clouds and the promise of rain before morning. A new cold front was pushing in from the northwest. It had produced blizzard conditions over the Rockies, but by the time it arrived in the Hill Country, it would probably only bring sleet and temperatures that plunged to just below the freezing mark.

Fitting weather, Darlene decided, for the chill that had invaded her heart. Every step forward in solving the mystery seemed a step forward in proving that the friend she had come to Vaquero to help might not have been who he seemed.

Someone was seeking revenge against James McCord, and she had been dragged into it, become a victim, because of what she knew or what she had seen. Because of facts that she had chosen to erase from her memory—along with everything she knew about herself—rather than face.

It was so bizarre that it defied belief, and yet it had happened. Clint had been at his computer or on his telephone almost every minute since they had returned from the Altamira, checking on facts and figures from the time span they'd pinpointed in McCord's old letters. And once again he had shut her out, refused her offers of assistance. She felt as invisible to him as her past life had become to her.

She picked up a section of newspaper Clint had tossed onto the coffee table that morning. The pages were crowded with seasonal sales. Only a few days left until the biggest gift-giving day of the year.

Christmas. The concept seemed foreign. She knew the holiday, what it stood for, how it was celebrated. Knew it impersonally and from a distance, the way she knew everything in her life.

Everything and everyone, except Clint Richards. Danger, amnesia, fear. In the face of all of that, she'd still fallen hopelessly in love with him. Or more likely, she'd never fallen out of love with him. The feelings had found a way through barriers that kept her memories hidden. All they had needed was a look, a touch, a kiss.

From the very beginning she had sensed that they had been far more than friends, knew even before he admitted it that they had been lovers. Now they were lovers again. Lovers, but not partners. He told her only what he decided she should know. Shared only the part of his life he chose to share.

She knew so little about herself, and yet she was certain she could never bear to be an outsider with the man she loved.

"You look like you might have run into a dead end," she said, turning from her view of the flames that frolicked in the stone fireplace to find him staring into space.

"I was just thinking about what I told Freddie Caulder, and wondering if he got my message to McCord."

"Do you think McCord will call if he did?"

"He might. If Caulder actually tells him I need to talk to him."

"You sound like Thornton Roberts. You're not beginning to doubt Freddie Caulder too, are you?"

"I doubt everyone's motives, right now. The more I try to make sense of this, the more it doesn't add up. Why would any man wait thirty years and then risk murder to seek revenge?"

"Maybe he didn't know where to find McCord until the press started dogging his every move."

"No, the ranch has been in the McCord family forever. He would have been easy to track down."

"I was thinking about Leon's description of the man he'd had the run-in with outside Bledsoe's ranch."

"It wasn't much of one." Clint picked up a stack of loose computer sheets and clipped them together.

"Middle-aged, graying, near six-feet tall. I know it sounds far-fetched, but Thornton Roberts would fit that description."

Clint nodded. "He was the first person I thought of. I faxed a picture of Thornton to the sheriff over in Prairie. He took the photo out to Leon's house and had him take a look at it. Leon said the man he'd seen was heavier, and that his hair had been a lot darker—a kind of salt-and-pepper. At any rate, he was certain Thornton was not the man."

"Is there a chance Leon would lie to protect himself? That he was just afraid that if he identified the man, he would come after him?"

"An outside chance. That's why I went ahead and ran yet another check on Thornton's background. I can't find anything to tie him to McCord before he signed on as security supervisor. And he was never in any branch of the armed services."

Clint tapped his pen on the pad and then bounced it across his desk. "Bits and pieces, but not quite enough to fit the puzzle together.'' His chair clattered against the tile floor as he pushed it back from his desk and stood up.

"Maybe you should take a break."

"I would, but my mind will never let me." He rubbed the back of his neck, stretching out the kinks. "I'm having another cup of coffee. Would you like one?"

"I'd never sleep tonight."

"I'll never sleep anyway."

Her eyes followed him until he'd disappeared through the kitchen door. She loved the way he walked, the way he smiled—even the way he frowned and stared into space when he was deep in thought. Loved the way he fit into the life he'd chosen for himself.

Even though he was out of her sight now, she could hear the cacophony from the kitchen and could visualize him warming his coffee on top of the range. No electric pot to brew his beverage of choice. He made it the old-fashioned way, dripping the boiling water over an abundance of dark crushed beans and then letting it steep over a low gas flame. He was a man grounded in the ways of the Hill Country where he'd grown up, yet he blended the old ways with technology to fight crime.

He knew the people he served, their weaknesses, their strengths. He knew who to push to the limit and who to coddle to get what he wanted from them. Yet, his computers at home and at his office were on the cutting edge, allowing him to track down the latest data from millions of files with the *click* of a hand-held mouse.

And everything about him, from the unruly shock of dark hair that defied attempts to control it to the scuffed toes of his western work boots, appealed to her sense of honor and order in a world gone haywire.

Even now, when she sensed they were running out of

time, and when she feared the images from the other night were not a figment of her drug-affected imagination but the memory of facts buried in her subconscious, she longed to go to him and bury herself in his arms.

But if she did that, she'd only prolong the inevitable. She had to get a few things settled between them. Needed to find out if there was a chance for them to make it work this time. If not, when she left tomorrow, it would be goodbye.

"Come and sit by me, Clint." Her voice was soft and strained, betraying the emotion and the strength of conviction that drove her.

He stretched and took another sip of his coffee. "I have another file to search, another list of casualties during the time period in question."

"It can wait a few minutes."

He relented, easing to the floor beside her, stretching his long legs in the direction of the fire. She shifted over to share the oversize pillow she'd propped against the back of the couch.

The aroma from his cup of coffee floated upwards, blending with the pungent odor of burning wood and the spicy fragrance of a bayberry candle she'd lit and placed on the hearth.

"Have we spent nights like this before, Clint, just you and me, sharing a warm fire on a chilly evening?"

"No." He stared into the fire. "But we swam naked in a spring-fed pool. At least, I tried to swim. You jumped on my back and dunked me." He touched her nose with his fingertip, teasing. "You were vicious."

She knew he was trying to keep the mood light, but she couldn't play his game—not tonight. "I envy you the memories of the time we were together."

He picked up his coffee cup and stared into it as if it

held magical answers. When he didn't find them, he lifted
the cup to his mouth and took a long, slow sip. "Your
memory will return. In the meantime, don't create fan-
tasies of happy-ever-after. They may come back to torment you."

"Is that why you're shutting me out, Clint, because
you're afraid that letting me in to your life will lead to
torment?"

"I don't know what you're talking about."

"Then answer a few questions for me."

He pulled away from the pillow they shared and sat
Indian-style beside her. "Fire away."

"It was you who spread the rumor that I had suffered
irreparable damage in the attack and that my memory was
never coming back, wasn't it?" She watched him tense
and knew how he hated to get into these confrontations.
But this time she wasn't going to back down. "Just answer me, Clint. It's easy. I ask a question. You answer
with the truth."

"I don't want us to fight." He slid his arm about her
shoulder.

"Talking isn't fighting."

"Then why does it always seem that way?"

"It wouldn't. If you'd just be completely honest with
me."

He exhaled and swallowed hard. "Okay, I told Dr.
Bennigan to spread the rumor. I decided that if the killer
thought you were never going to remember anything, he
wouldn't be as desperate to kill you. I thought it would
buy us a little time before he struck again." His fingers
tangled in her hair. "I was trying to protect you. That's
all."

"So why didn't you just tell me that? Instead, I had

to hear it from people who'd picked it up third-hand from the streets.''

''You were supposed to leave town in a day or two. I didn't see any reason to bother you with it.''

''The same way you didn't see any reason to ask me how I felt about flying back to D.C. tomorrow morning?''

He threw up his hands in exasperation. ''My job is to protect you.''

''I'm an adult, Clint. An FBI agent. I don't have a memory, but I have a brain. I can make decisions about my own life, especially if we talk about the issues, examine the dangers together.''

''I have work to do, Darlene. We'll talk later.'' He stood up and walked back to his desk.

She followed him. ''No. I'm leaving in the morning, remember?''

''They have telephones in D.C. I'll call you.''

''I don't think so, Clint. If we can't talk about important issues when we're together, then we certainly can't deal with them over miles of cable.''

She was hurting inside, knowing she was delivering ultimatums that she would have to live with forever. She didn't want to lose Clint, but if he didn't trust her enough to share his life with her, she'd already lost him. Probably the same way she'd lost him before, though it obviously wasn't the way he'd chosen to view their breakup.

''The truth, Clint. That's all I ask. About the little issues and the big ones.''

''Fine. The truth is, I deliberately made the decision to spread the rumor about your amnesia not being reversible.'' He stepped in front of the window and stared into the darkness. ''I made a mistake. I should have asked you before I did it, the same way I should have asked you if you wanted to go back to D.C. But if I had, you would have said no to both questions. And I can't take a chance with your life.'' Agony tore at his voice.

It would be so easy to step into his arms, to hold onto him until the quaking fear inside her melted away. But she couldn't.

''Why did you lie to me tonight, Clint? Why did you tell me you didn't recognize the woman in the picture with McCord? My life wasn't in danger over that.''

''Because it didn't matter.'' He stuck his hand on the window frame and leaned into it, still directing his gaze into the night, and away from her.

''If it hadn't mattered, you would have told me the truth. If you *trusted* me, you would have told me the truth. The way it is now, I feel as if you're deliberately holding a shield between us so that I can't get too close to you.''

She stood at his elbow, but didn't touch him. And even the sky seemed to react to the tension that hovered between them. Slivers of lightning darted around and through dark, threatening clouds. The silence grew ominous, the invisible abyss between them growing wider and deeper with each passing second of silence.

But still she couldn't give up on him. Not yet. She had to see if he could open up to her and share the feelings that shaped his life, that ruled his very existence. If he couldn't, there was no way they could make it together, no matter how much they loved each other.

''What is there between you and McCord that tears you apart, Clint? Half the time you speak his name as if it were poison on your tongue. Tonight you wouldn't even admit that the woman in the picture with McCord was your mother. And yet, I sense you're worried about him.''

"I'm the sheriff. My job is to protect everyone in my district. Even McCord."

"You're avoiding the question." She stepped nearer, until she was so close she could all but feel the pressures grappling inside him. "Did you resent my friendship with him? Resent the fact that he could give me things you couldn't, that he helped me get that appointment at Quantico? Because if you've harbored that kind of enmity over no more than that, then you're not the man I think you are. Not the man I fell in love with."

He turned around to face her, and she trembled at the anguish that burned in his dark eyes. "I love you, Darlene. But I can't change who I am. No more than I could six years ago."

"I'm not asking you to change. I'm only asking you to trust me with your feelings and not shut me out of your life."

Her voice was shaking. She was shaking. But her only chance to find happiness with the man she loved depended on breaking through the barriers, depended on him trusting her with his secrets the way he wanted her to trust him with her life. And she might never get this close to reaching him again.

"We love each other, Clint. We could make it work. But you have to let me in to your life."

He turned and stamped toward the back door. She watched him go, defeat so heavy in her heart that she couldn't even stand alone. She slumped against the windowsill.

Clint stopped just inside the back door, his hat in his hand. "You want the truth? I'll give it to you." His voice was strained, yet hard and unrelenting. "I did resent your friendship with McCord. Yours and every other person's in this town. He was Mr. Wonderful to everyone in Star County. To everyone except me.''

Clint slammed his hat on his head and swung open the screen door. ''I had McCord on a pedestal so high he would have needed an oxygen tank to breathe. But he never cared. Never wanted me around. Either I wasn't good enough for him, or else every time he looked at me he was reminded of the one mistake he couldn't make completely disappear.''

She felt the pain in his voice deep in her soul. ''What are you saying, Clint?''

''That I'm James McCord's bastard son.''

The door slammed so fiercely behind him that the house shook from the impact. She crossed the floor and leaned against the door, half of her wanting to go after Clint, the smarter half knowing he needed the time to himself.

But she could no longer hold back the tears that she'd fought through days of frustration and fear. Sobbing, and for once not caring, she dropped to the couch and buried her face in the cushions.

JAMES MCCORD DIALED Clint's home number for the tenth time. Still no answer. But Caulder had said Clint was furious and demanding that McCord call him at home tonight.

The phones were probably out again. The lines had probably been knocked down by a tree limb, the way that north wind was gusting. Or maybe by lightning damage. The last round of fiery bolts had been vertical, aimed straight for the earth.

He dropped his borrowed cell phone to the empty passenger seat of the borrowed truck. He was damn tired of being a fugitive, not even trusting the people who'd been hired to protect him. Living on the run from a lunatic who was threatening to destroy everything he'd worked so hard to build. Worst of all, threatening the lives of people he loved.

First, it had been his daughter. Thankfully, Levi was safe now and thousands of miles away, but the madman had turned his hate and vengeance to Darlene. And now that Clint was getting so close to the truth, he was sure to be next on the death list.

Clint.

McCord tensed as the fury inside him mingled with regret. He should never have made that vow to Eileen, should never have promised to deny his own son his name. Should never have denied himself his son. And yet he knew if he had to do it all over again, it wouldn't be any different.

No matter that he'd loved her, that she'd been the woman who'd taught him how to love, how to face life after the shattering injury had claimed his leg. She was his best friend's wife, and neither of them had been willing to throw that kind of painful baggage on a man who had just lived through hell.

But Eileen was dead now, and so was the man they had lied to protect. And if the lunatic who had sent him the threatening letters had his way, McCord might soon be dead too. And he would die without once hearing his son call him Dad.

His hands tightened on the wheel as he swerved and made the turn onto the road that led to Clint's ranch. He wouldn't break his vow to Eileen. That was sacred. But he would have to break a promise he'd made years ago to a group of buddies in a distant land. He'd broken it once, the night he'd told Darlene.

When the story was out, it would end any chance of

his being elected president, any chance of his ever being involved in politics again. It might lose him the respect of his family. It might even cost him his freedom.

But he had no choice, just as he'd had no choice thirty years ago when he'd pulled a trigger and killed his commanding officer. A man did what he had to do.

CLINT STOOD IN THE STABLES, just inside the door where he still had a view of the house. He rubbed Brandy's long neck, getting what comfort he could from the smell of horseflesh, the feel of dirt and straw under his feet, the sound of snorting and whinnying as the animals reacted to the storm.

Sounds, smells, sights that were the substance of his existence. Yet tonight they didn't quell the rumblings in his soul. He'd blamed Darlene and McCord for the loneliness he'd endured the last six years, blamed them even as he'd denied that he was lonely. And he'd denied to himself that he was half a man without Darlene, that he would never stop loving her as long as he drew breath.

But any way you cut it, the fault had all been his. He'd sat on the edge of the bed, holding his mother's hand when she'd told him that James McCord was his real father. Then she'd closed her eyes, never to open them again.

In that second, his whole conception of who he was had changed. The man he'd thought had been his father wasn't. Instead, he'd been conceived from the seed of the national hero he'd grown up worshiping—the man who had turned away every time Clint had tried to get close to him, stinging him with rejection even a kid could feel, but not understand.

That night had been the beginning of the end of him and Darlene. She had called it right tonight, the same way she had called it right back then. He wasn't the man she'd fallen in love with.

But she was back in his life again, and he'd be damned if he'd let his reactions to the past rob him of the chance to spend his life with the woman he loved.

She could still walk away when this was over and her amnesia was resolved. She could go back to her career and the life she'd made for herself. But she'd leave knowing he loved her as much as any man had ever loved a woman. He owed her that.

THE WIND HAD PICKED UP, whirling leaves and making missiles of dirt and debris as Clint headed back to the house. He held his hat with one hand and protected his eyes with the other as he crossed the space between the stables and the house. A hell of a night out for man or beast. Even Darlene's would-be killer was probably huddling beside a fire tonight.

A vicious bolt of lightning made the night as light as day, and a thundering crash of thunder followed. Clint broke into a jog, hoping to reach the house before the rain started.

The crashing *smack* of wood on wood slowed him. He couldn't see much in the dark, but he recognized the sound. The wind was playing with his barn door— blowing it open one minute only to hurl it shut the next.

He'd thought for sure he'd latched it earlier, but evidently he hadn't. He'd have to make a quick detour and take care of it. He didn't keep that much in the old barn: some hay, feed for the cattle, a few tools. But the way the wind was blowing tonight, what he had would get soaked if he left that door flapping.

He broke into a full-fledged run and didn't stop until he'd stepped under the roof of the barn and grabbed hold of the edge of the swinging door. He lifted and pulled against the wind. He'd almost done it when he felt the glancing blow to his head and stumbled backward.

Right into the barrel of a gun.

Chapter Fifteen

"Hello, Clint. Nice of you to stop by. I figured you'd come to check on that banging door sooner or later. I had no idea it would be this soon."

"Thornton, what are you doing in my barn?"

"Like I said, waiting for you." He shoved the gun into the recess between his shoulder blades. "Don't make any foolish moves, Clint. Don't give me an excuse to pull this trigger before I'm ready."

"If I'm going to take a bullet anyway, now's as good as later to me." But he wasn't stupid enough to call Thornton's bluff. Thornton reached down and yanked Clint's revolver from its holster and tossed it to the middle of the barn.

Clint kept his cool. He had to be alert. Weapon or no, he still had a chance to save himself and warn Darlene. The chance lessened when Thornton pulled a pair of cuffs from his back pocket and fastened the steel bracelets around Clint's wrists. Thornton reached behind him with one hand and flicked on the dim overhead light.

"Darlene's probably wandering where you are. If she looks out here and sees the light, she might save me the trouble of going after her."

"You're wasting your time," Clint lied. "She left with

Randy a few minutes ago. He was driving her to San Antonio to catch a flight to D.C.''

"No, I talked to Whitt Emory not more than an hour ago. He has her protection all lined up starting the second she steps off the plane *tomorrow*."

"So you decided to outsmart him. Get to her here where you only had me to walk over."

"And you made it so easy." He shoved Clint toward the center of the barn.

Clint moved without resistance. The longer he kept Thornton busy with him, the better Darlene's chances were at staying alive. If she came out into the dark looking for him, she'd bring a gun. If Thornton went into the house looking for her, she might not even have a fighting chance.

"Back up against that post, Clint."

"So are you going to tell me what this is about?" he asked, following Thornton's orders. "What's your reason for hating McCord?"

"Justice. It's been thirty years in coming. But I'll die before I see the man who shot my brother Hal in cold blood become the president of the United States."

Realization hit like a ton of bricks, and Clint recoiled under the weight of it. He tried to put together what he'd learned from the files at the Altamira and the data he'd been able to access on his computer. Hal Edwards. Known to his buddies as Whacko. He'd been on the A-Team with McCord. He'd been the commanding officer of the mission that had taken place during the crucial time period Darlene had identified this afternoon. He had not returned from the mission.

This must have been the horrifying story McCord had shared with Darlene on Monday night. She'd learned that McCord was a murderer.

"You don't have to kill Darlene to make your own justice, Thornton. Her amnesia is permanent. She'll never be able to identify you from the attack."

Thornton laughed, a nervous cackle that bordered on hysteria. "She'll never be able to identify me because she never saw me. I wore a ski mask and a flowing cloak that disguised my physique. And I never said one word, so there was not even a minute chance someone could recognize my voice. I'm the best at what I do, Sheriff, just like you. Only *I* don't make mistakes."

"Then let Darlene go. Why kill an innocent woman?"

"Because she's not an innocent woman. She's with the FBI. I knew she'd be a problem from the beginning. That's why I was prepared to take her out the day she set foot in Vaquero. Like you, she won't stop until she implicates me in the attack and McCord's murder."

"McCord hasn't been murdered."

"He will be. Take my word for it. You, Darlene, McCord. It's too late for all of you."

"You'll never get away with this."

"Yes, I will. That's the beauty of it. The identity and background I created for myself are flawless. Jake Edwards died in a boating accident. I'm now Thornton Roberts, security expert from Minnesota. No one will question that."

"They will when McCord shows up dead."

"No. Not the way I have his murder planned. Not once you and Darlene are no longer alive to thwart me."

"Leave Darlene out of this, Jake. She can't hurt you. The part of her brain that controls her memory was permanently damaged. She will never remember what McCord told her."

"I'm not willing to take that chance. Now I have to hurry. I'm going to tie you to the center post. I'll have to remove the cuffs so that none of this will ever be tied to me. If you make the slightest attempt to escape, I'll shoot you.''

Clint had no doubt that Jake Edwards meant exactly what he said. The man's eyes shone with the glassy sheen of a madman's, and his trigger finger was poised and ready.

Clint's chances were running out. And he couldn't just sit back and do nothing. He stood against the post, compliant, waiting until the exact second when his left hand was free of the cuff.

He jerked with all his might, breaking loose and diving to the ground. He slid across the carpet of loose straw, the tips of his fingers mere inches from the butt of his revolver—

The sound of gunfire reverberated like thunder through the narrow barn.

Jake Edwards's bullet had found its mark.

DARLENE HAD CRIED herself out, then got up and washed the mascara from her face. She'd even warmed some packages of homemade soup she'd found in the freezer, no doubt provided by friendly neighbors. It would be the only supper they'd need after Mary's Sunday dinner. The table was set. The ice in the tea glasses had started to melt.

But Clint had not returned.

He was close by. He would never leave her unprotected, no matter how angry he was that she'd pushed him so hard and so far. The secret he'd guarded so fiercely had been more brutal than she'd expected, but she wasn't sorry she'd kept at him until he'd exploded with the truth.

It was a jaggedly scarred beginning, but it was a beginning for them. The barriers Clint had erected between them had started to topple, and they had started with the foundation of steel. The rest would be easier.

Now she just wished Clint would walk back through the door.

The zigzagging spikes of lightning had become almost constant, quickly followed by ear-splitting crashes of thunder that exploded like gunfire. The rain would start soon. Probably come down in torrents if the preview was any indication.

If Clint didn't return in a few minutes, she'd go looking for him. He shouldn't be out on a night like this. Loopy lifted his head, his ears jumping to attention.

"You're worried about him too, aren't you, boy?" She reached down to offer a reassuring pat, but Loopy sprang to his feet and took off for the back door, barking an agitated greeting. Darlene's hands flew to her hair, straightening it into place. Clint must finally have decided to face her again.

The back door flew open, but it wasn't Clint who stepped inside.

"Thornton, what are you doing here?"

"I came to see Clint."

"He's outside. I'll get him."

"I found him already, Darlene. He's out in the barn, and he's hurt. You better come with me."

"Is he…"

"He's alive, but he's hurt bad. Looks like he slipped from the top of the ladder and fell. He can't move his legs, though, and he's asking for you."

The room began to spin around her. No wonder Clint hadn't come back. She should have known something was wrong. She should have checked sooner. Hands shaking, she grabbed the phone to call for an ambulance, but the line was dead—knocked out by the raging storm.

"Get your car, Thornton. You can drive it right up to the barn. We have to get Clint to the hospital." She rushed past him, flying down the back steps and running against a driving wind that tore at her clothes and whipped her hair into her mouth and eyes.

Thornton was right behind her, and not in his car as she'd asked. A wave of suspicion rolled through her mind. Thornton had never been to the ranch before. Why would he be here now? How would he have found Clint injured in the barn?

Reasoning collided with the fear that raced through her senses. She was running as fast as she could, but she might be racing into a trap that would get her and Clint killed.

She swung around and started back toward the house. Thornton grabbed her arm and jerked her to a stop. "Where do you think you're going?"

"To get first aid supplies." She tried to appear calm, to convince him she'd be right back. Which she would be—only this time she'd have a gun. "There might be something I can do before we get Clint to the hospital."

"I don't think so. He won't be going to a hospital. There won't even be enough left of him to take to the morgue."

Thornton's expression, as much as his cruel words, ripped her apart. A trap. She'd been right, only not soon enough.

"Start walking again, Darlene. Your sheriff lover is waiting for you."

"It's me you're looking for, Thornton. Not Clint. He doesn't know anything. He can't hurt you."

"He does now. He knows I shot him and tied him up

so that he could wait for your arrival." He shoved her, the gun bumping against her body with every step.

If she ran, he'd pull the trigger. If she didn't, he would kill her anyway. But if Clint was in the barn, they might be able to do something together. And if Thornton was lying, then Clint was out there somewhere and he would save her.

This was no time to give up. She slowed her step, and Thornton kicked her from behind, sending her stumbling into the door of the barn. It flew open, and he dragged her inside. But now the barrel of the gun had moved from her ribs to the tender area of her temple, just below the bandage.

"Okay, Clint," he announced, his voice echoing from the rafters. "The guest of honor at our party has arrived. The celebrity barn-burning can commence."

Darlene struggled to break from Thornton's grasp, to rush to Clint. His hands and feet were tied behind his back, and his left leg below the knee was a bloody mass. He looked at her and smiled, but she only saw his pain and the paleness of his face.

Thornton yanked her arm behind her back, and ground the pistol into her head. She kicked at him, and he twisted her arm even farther, until she thought it might break.

"Don't fight him, Darlene. He's a madman."

"I don't understand." She turned from Thornton to Clint. "Tell me what's going on."

"It's easy to understand," Clint said, the bitterness drawing his voice to a husky low, "once you know the real identities of the players. Thornton's real name is Jake Edwards. He's Whacko's brother. Apparently crazy is a family trait."

"Shut up, Clint." Jake threw his arm over Darlene,

catching her neck in a vise grip between his forearm and his body. "I've heard enough from you."

"So it was you. And Leon lied to protect himself."

"I don't know what you're talking about." He dragged Darlene toward the ladder that led to the loft, right past a bale of hay. For one brief second she fastened her gaze on the hay rake that rested against the bale and then looked away, not wanting to alert Thornton that she'd noticed it.

And just a few yards ahead of her was Clint's gun, shoved against a spare tractor tire. If there were only some way she could break loose. But Thornton's hold on her was too tight. He was too strong. And the barrel of his gun was still at her temple.

The lights in the barn flickered, and for one terrifying instant the barn was bathed in total darkness. In that second the barn door flew open, letting in a blast of cold mist and sending loose blades of hay dancing around her feet.

Jake spat out, "What the—"

Darlene turned, and her heart plunged to her stomach.

"McCord." The name slipped off her tongue as the man standing in the door took in the scene and went for his gun.

"Drop the gun, Thornton, and let Darlene go."

"I knew that amnesia story was a bunch of bull." Jake tightened his grip on Darlene's neck. "You seem to remember McCord well enough."

He was right. The second McCord had spoken, she'd known who he was. She had been with him, a few nights ago, sitting on the front of his truck. He'd lit his pipe.

The memories rushed into her head. Still confusing, still hazy, but they were there. The amnesia was fading. But was it too late to matter?

"Drop the gun, Thornton," McCord ordered. "And then you can tell me what this is about."

"James McCord, meet Jake Edwards," Clint said, "brother of the late Hal Edwards, an old war buddy of yours."

McCord's face registered surprise and then shock. He held his gun in front of him, one hand ready to pull the trigger, one holding the barrel steady and pointed right at Jake's head.

"Drop the gun or I'll shoot, Jake. You know me. I'll do it."

"I'm not dropping anything. If I die, Darlene dies. And then you'll have to kill Clint the way you killed Hal, or he'll tell the world the ugly truth about you."

"You don't even know the truth." McCord spit the words at the man who'd eaten at his table, drunk his wine, and pretended to be his protector.

"I know the truth, all right," Jake countered. "You killed my brother in cold blood, and you did it in front of six other men. That's how audacious you were. You were so sure your friends would stand behind you, so sure you would get away with it. Only one person talked. And he named you as the hit man."

"You've got it all wrong, Jake." McCord kept up his chatter, buying time. "Hal was killed while on a mission. Your brother died a hero. That's the way his death was reported. Don't muddy his reputation now."

"Shut up, you old fool. You can't sway me. Not when I've waited so long. Besides, there was never any glory, not for Hal. He didn't come waltzing home to have a big shiny medal pinned on him."

"I didn't come 'waltzing' home." McCord lifted his prosthesis, balancing on his one good leg. "I came *hobbling* home."

"And you were just about to hobble up the steps to the White House. The people's choice to lead them into the twenty-first century. Only you're not going to make it. I'm not going to let you make it."

"Do you want me to take my name out of the hat, Jake? I can do that. I *will* do that. Let Darlene and Clint go, and we'll talk."

"It's too late now, McCord. Thirty years too late."

"What makes you think I killed your brother?"

"I don't think it. I *know* it."

"You weren't there. You were rotting away in some jail in Kansas for holding up a liquor store. The man who told you I shot Hal was lying."

"Nice try, but I also heard the words right out of your mouth. The night you told it to Darlene on Glenn Road."

"You couldn't have."

"I could and I did. You were wired."

"No way. The truck might have been, but we got out of the truck. There was no way to have me wired."

"There was a way." This time it was Clint who was talking. "Jake planted the bug in your wallet—the one we found at the scene of the crime. The forensics boys picked up the indentation. They notified me by e-mail a little while ago."

"Give it up, McCord. Drop the gun. Or the babe here gets it first. At the count of three. One, two…"

Darlene heard the metallic *click* as Jake cocked the pistol.

"Drop it, McCord," Clint ordered. "He's not bluffing."

McCord dropped his gun onto the floor, but for a second Darlene thought he was going to lunge for Jake. Instead, he straightened and held his position close to the door.

"Do you really think killing any of us is worth spending the rest of your life in jail, Jake? Why don't you just go to the people with the truth," Clint taunted, still not giving up. "Let them see for themselves what a sorry bastard McCord is. Hell, better than that, you can sell the story to one of the tabloids and make a fortune for yourself."

Jake kicked the post Clint was tied to. "You take me for a fool, don't you? All of you." His voice was rising, louder and higher, straining so that his words slurred. He was going over the edge. They'd pushed him too far.

"Get against that post to the left of you, McCord." Jake picked up a length of rope and tossed it at McCord's feet, ordering Darlene to pick it up and bind the senator's hands.

"Do what he says, Darlene," Clint urged. "This isn't over yet."

When she'd tied the knot to suit Jake, he dragged her to the stud nearest Clint. The rope was already in place, dangling and curling around the post like a snake ready to strike.

He let go of her arm and grabbed her around the neck again, this time squeezing so tightly she couldn't breathe. She struggled and gasped, the way she had done the other night in the hospital. Only he'd never be able to hold her like that and tie a rope around her hands.

She focused on the gun. She'd have to find a way to get closer.

"Don't try to get *loose,* Darlene." Clint was pleading with her. She met his gaze. He was trying to signal her, but she had no idea what he wanted her to do.

She lunged, but went nowhere. Jake was already pulling the knot tight around her wrists. He stooped and tied her feet to the post as well, before he walked to the ladder that led to the loft. Climbing up the first few rungs, he stretched to the opening and retrieved a palm-size recorder.

"I think you'll all find this interesting. You most of all, McCord, though I had no idea you'd be here for tonight's performance. This along with the double murder/suicide note I'll leave in a perfect imitation of McCord's handwriting will more than satisfy the police and the media. Especially since everyone in town will back up the fact that Clint and Darlene have been investigating McCord." He flipped a switch, and the barn was filled with sound.

The voice was McCord's. The Texas accent, the rough cowboy edge, the euphemisms. Unmistakably James McCord. He was apologizing to the American people for lying to them, for letting them believe he was a hero when he had disgraced the country so flagrantly.

"I've never said anything like that," McCord said. "That can't be my voice."

But it was his voice, taken from other tapes and forged into a product that no one would doubt. Jake Edwards's technology had bonded with evil for the perfect crime. They would all die, and McCord would be blamed.

Jake Edwards would walk away a free man.

His raucous laughter filled the barn as he reached into the pocket of his jeans and pulled out a silver lighter. "I'm going to be leaving now, but I won't leave you in the cold. I'm going to start a fire to warm you."

"You should have brought some fireworks," Clint snarled. "Made a party out of this. After all, you waited thirty years to get your sick revenge."

But Darlene couldn't take it as well as Clint could. She didn't want to die. She wanted to live. She wanted to make love with Clint and have his children.

"Why, Jake, why?" Darlene begged through the shudders of fear that shook her as Jake touched the flickering lighter to the dry hay. "Can't you just shoot us—at least be human enough to let us die quickly? You'd do that much for an animal. Can't you do it for us?"

Jake walked over to stand in front of McCord. "This is the man who can answer that question for you." He started a new fire and fanned the smoke toward McCord's slumped body. McCord coughed as the smoke surrounded his face.

"But ask him quick, Darlene. He's already coughing his last breaths away."

Darlene closed her eyes as the smoke curled around her face and seeped into her lungs. "I love you, Clint," she said, her voice shaky and hoarse. If he answered her, she didn't hear him over the crackle of the spot fires that sprang to life all around them. Couldn't hear him over the hysterical laugh of a madman as he slammed the door of the barn behind him and dropped the heavy latch into place.

Chapter Sixteen

"Hold still, Darlene. I don't want to cut you with my pocketknife on top of everything else."

For a second she thought she was dreaming. She opened her eyes. Clint was at her back, sawing away on the chunky rope that held her to the post.

"How did you get untied?"

"Jake's high tech, but he's not a rancher. Those knots couldn't hold a newborn calf."

"They could unless the calf was named Houdini." She blinked back tears. She wasn't sure if they were from relief or from smoke, and she didn't really care. "I tried to get loose," she said. "My ropes only held tighter."

He pulled down the protective mask he'd made from his shirt and kissed her, a quick peck on the lips. "Don't talk. Save your breath." He returned to the task of cutting, not slowing or speaking again until the rope gave and her hands broke free.

She shook them vigorously, the sudden, rapid circulation creating a tingling sensation that ran up and down her arms. She sucked in a ragged breath and realized how close she'd come to giving up on life.

"Take off your shirt and cover your mouth while I get the ankles." Clint half coughed the words, but he didn't hesitate to bend low into the dense smoke to finish the task. Darlene rubbed her eyes and searched through the thickening smoke for McCord, as Clint sawed through the tough rope at her ankles with the thin blade of his pocketknife.

Finally the last ends were cut clean, and she kicked the loose rope from her feet. "I can't locate McCord," she whispered, her voice so hoarse she could barely hear it herself. "The fire is worse toward the door."

"I'll get him. You head for the loft."

"No, I'm not going without you. I'll follow you to McCord."

He ignored her offer, tugging her toward the ladder.

"We have to help him, Clint," Darlene pleaded. "We can't leave him to die." Her voice sputtered in the black smoke. She tried to yank away from Clint, but she was no match for his strength.

"Get up the steps, Darlene. *Now.* Don't turn back, no matter what you see or hear. And use this if you have to." He pressed his revolver into her hand and shoved her into the ladder. "Now climb!"

"No. Not without you and McCord."

"It's too late to save McCord. He's by the door where Jake concentrated his fire-setting effort. Go to the windows and swing them open. Then close your eyes and jump. Don't think. Just jump!" He held her close one last time before pushing her away. "Now climb. I'm right behind you."

She slipped on the top rung and turned to grab hold of him, but he wasn't there, just his voice yelling at her over the crackle of flames that had now taken hold and were leaping toward her. She stopped, terrified, yet determined to find him.

"Jump, Darlene. You're our best chance."

New flames erupted behind her, so close that the heat scorched her skin. She stopped at the window and called for Clint. This time there was no answer. But she didn't wonder where he was.

He had gone back for McCord. Like father, like son. Heroes to the end.

She closed her eyes and jumped. If you can't beat 'em, join 'em. She would find a way to save them.

Or die trying.

CLINT FOUGHT HIS WAY through the flames, dodging fiery beams that burned loose and came crashing down around him. He found McCord and fell to the ground beside him. The older man wasn't moving but he was breathing, heavy jagged breaths that still hadn't provided the oxygen to keep him fully conscious.

Clint slashed at the ropes, pressing as hard as he could. Fortunately, the snatch of rope Jake had used on McCord was thinner than the one he had used on Clint and Darlene. It responded more quickly to the sharp edge of the knife.

The second the rope broke free, Clint fit his hands beneath McCord's shoulders. He could barely stand himself without his knee buckling under him, but he no longer felt the jabbing stabs of pain where the bullet had shattered his flesh. He was too numb from the smoke and the effort to breathe.

"You've got to help me, McCord. I can't do this by myself." He could taste the panic swelling inside him. He was tired, weak. If he could just rest a minute...

No. He couldn't think like that. If he stopped, it would be the end for both of them. Sweat poured down his face, rolling into his eyes and mouth. He tugged, but McCord didn't budge.

Mustering his last reserves of strength, he slapped McCord hard across the face. He had to bring him to, had to have the man's help or they would never make it up to the loft and out the window. And there was no other way out. The door was completely engulfed in flames.

Their chances were almost nil, with the flames turning the area around the ladder into ribbons of fire and falling timbers. But he had to try.

He shook McCord as hard as he could, and this time McCord shifted and groaned. "Put your arm around my neck," he urged, his throat so dry he could barely form the words. "You have to help me."

"I can't. Go without me, Clint. I'll only slow you down."

"I can't leave you. You know that. We make it together, or we don't make it."

Clint tried to see the loft. He couldn't. The flames were shooting up all around it. Even if he had the strength to carry McCord, they couldn't make it now. He collapsed beside him.

"You had to know we didn't have a prayer," McCord rasped. "Why did you come back for me?"

"I don't know." Clint slumped over on McCord, his arm still slung around his shoulder. "I guess I couldn't just leave my *dad* to die without trying to save him."

"What did you say?"

"I said...*Dad.*"

McCord buried his face in Clint's arms. "This is a hell of a time to find out you know the truth. A hell of a way to find and then lose a son."

They were both coughing now. And crying. Or maybe it was just the smoke.

Clint closed his eyes and thought of Darlene. She'd

wanted him to share his life. Now he wasn't going to have one to share. He only hoped she knew how much he loved her. He covered his head with his arm as the fire crackled around him and the flames got closer—

The barn suddenly shook violently around him, knocking him backward. He straightened and then gasped in surprise as the wall behind him toppled and the hood of his pickup pushed its way inside.

Darlene had found a way.

Adrenaline spurted through him, aided by the new supply of oxygen that rolled through the hole the truck had made. Darlene jumped out of the driver's door and rushed toward them.

Darlene Remington, FBI agent to the rescue. Torn clothes, wet hair, tear-stained face. And no one had ever looked so good.

Together they dragged McCord to the truck and pushed him into the passenger side. Clint climbed in beside him, and Darlene jumped behind the wheel, backing away from the building just as the other side of the barn gave way and the remainder of the roof crashed to the ground in front of them.

"Next time you tell me to catch a plane out of Vaquero, I'll take you up on it," she said, swerving the truck into a 360-degree turn.

"Sorry, lady." Clint reached across McCord and managed a weak high-five, linking fingers and holding on. "You missed your chance at leaving. I'm not making that mistake again."

Darlene tried the turn again, this time winding up headed in the right direction.

Heading home.

CLINT GLANCED AT THE CLOCK. It was pushing midnight, and they were just getting home from the emergency room. Darlene had to be as worn out as he was from the close call with death. And still dealing with the shock of finding the severely burned body of Jake Edwards a few feet from Clint's back steps.

The best they could figure, the man had lingered to make sure they didn't escape, or just to hear their cries as the fire took their lives. Only he'd stood too close. His clothes had apparently caught fire from a windblown spark, and he had taken off running for the house.

He'd never made it.

"Can I help you with that crutch?" Darlene asked, stepping in front of Clint to push a chair out of his path.

"I might as well learn to use it. Looks like I'll be stuck with it for a while." Clint leaned his crutch against the arm of the sofa and fell to the cushioned seat. Wincing at the sudden jab of pain, he eased his leg to the pillow Darlene had positioned on the coffee table.

"And this is for you," she said, pressing a skinny capsule into his hand. "One every four hours. And don't make that face. I'm just following doctor's orders."

"Oh, and when did you turn over this new leaf?"

"When you became the patient, of course."

He swallowed the pill, following the foul taste with a tall glass of water. One of many he'd downed tonight.

Darlene sat down on the coach next to him. "Is the pain bad?"

"I've had worse. Maybe."

"I'm just thankful the damage was no more serious than it was." She eyed the bandage that wrapped around his leg just below the knee. "Not that tearing apart flesh and muscle isn't bad. But Dr. Bennigan thinks you'll be back at work in a few weeks."

"I'll be back at work *tomorrow*, taking care of the

mounds of paperwork that go with winding up a case."
He draped an arm around her shoulders. "But I won't be
complaining about it. I'm just glad I'm alive to work."

He cupped her chin in his hand, and tilted her face
toward him. "I wouldn't have given McCord and me the
chance I'd give a calf in the slaughterhouse, until you
drove that truck through the wall." He kissed her lips,
and marveled at the thrill that danced through him in spite
of his weakened condition. "Guess I'll have to up my
opinion of the FBI."

"I'll take that compliment, cowboy." She snuggled
against his chest. "But it was you who gave me the
chance. I still don't understand how you managed to get
loose from that rope—but I'm grateful."

"I didn't do it with any time to spare."

"And I'm still not quite sure how McCord ended up
walking in on us in the barn," Darlene added, confusion
twisting her cute little mouth into a frown.

"Apparently, he'd talked to Caulder tonight and found
out that we'd been at the Altamira going through Mc-
Cord's old war paraphernalia. He was afraid we were
getting too close to the truth."

"And he decided to come clean, at least to you."

"He thought it might make me heed his warning about
not getting involved."

"Because he thought the investigation might get you
killed." Darlene ran her fingers over his hands. "And it
almost did."

"Almost got both of us killed." He took her hand in
his, gingerly rubbing his fingers along the bruises and
cuts from the rope that had bound her to the post. "I
went through hell and back more than once in that barn,
knowing what I had led you into."

"You didn't lead me into anything. We were in it together.'' She squeezed his hand and looked up at him, her eyes misty and soft. ''It was a big night for you. Not only fighting the fire, but letting go of your secret about your parentage. To me and to McCord.''

He swallowed hard and shifted uneasily. He'd spent the last six years resenting McCord for perceived shuns and worse. He'd been convinced McCord had come home from the war a hero, powerful and assured, the way he'd been for as far back as Clint could remember.

He'd imagined that McCord had taken advantage of his mother, charmed her right into his bed while her own husband had been imprisoned in a war camp. Consciously, he'd directed all his anger toward McCord because he had never been able to lay blame on his mom. But on another level, one that cut more deeply into his heart, he'd felt disillusioned by his mother's unfaithfulness to the only father he'd ever known. He'd felt she'd betrayed the both of them.

The story McCord had told him at the hospital tonight had been far different. It had been of two lonely, frightened young people. He'd come home minus one leg and tormented by the fact that he'd been forced to shoot his own officer. She was lonely, believing that her husband had died as reported instead of being taken prisoner.

McCord and his mother had begun as friends and had fallen in love. But in the end, they'd made decisions based on other people's needs, Clint's included.

''I guess I did a lot of growing up tonight,'' Clint said. ''That's not so easy for me to admit.''

Darlene fit her body more securely into the cradle of his arm. ''Admitting you're wrong is never easy. Will you be able to build a relationship with McCord?''

''I don't know, but at least I understand better what it was like for him and my mother. And I know that what

I perceived as put-downs were his way of keeping the vow he'd made to a woman he loved very much. I can't fault him for that.''

"I only wish he'd told me the whole story that night on Glenn Road before we were attacked. If I'd understood his reasons for doing what he did, I would have been able to deal with it. The whole amnesia problem might have been prevented."

"Still, it was a rough situation, a tough call to make. I wouldn't have wanted to be in McCord's shoes. But knowing him, I'm sure he wouldn't do it any differently if he had to make that same decision again." Clint rearranged his leg on the pillow, trying to find an angle that hurt less.

Darlene took up the story, as if clarifying it in her own mind. "Hal had already gotten two men killed by his reckless orders. And he was about to shoot the third for not walking into the same trap. McCord stepped in."

She bit her bottom lip, obviously still perplexed over the events that had led up to tonight. "I still don't see why Jake had become obsessed with setting the fire and having McCord die in the flames. Hal was already dead when they ignited the encampment. And that was not so much to destroy evidence of his murder as to hide from the enemy the fact that they had been there."

Clint tangled his fingers in Darlene's hair, and buried his lips at the nape of her beautiful neck. "I guess we'll never know why Jake reacted like he did. It's just sad that he let it eat away at him for thirty years."

"And he might still have done nothing, if he hadn't heard that Whitt Emory was looking to hire someone to head up security at the senator's ranch. With his experience and knowledge, he was a shoo-in for the job. All he had to do was create a fake identity."

"I'm sure Whitt will look a lot harder at the next man he hires," Clint said. "Though I'm sure Jake covered all the bases. He was a smart man. Too bad that intelligence couldn't have been used for good."

"I know. He claimed he only wanted justice. And then he died in the same way he meant for us to. A crueler punishment than the courts would ever have meted out for him."

Clint buried his mouth in the silky strands of Darlene's hair. The pill was taking effect, making his eyelids heavy, his thinking processes slow. He didn't want to talk of Jake or even McCord any more tonight. He only wanted to hold Darlene close. For as long as he could.

"It's nice to have my memories back," she whispered.

"Do you remember everything?" He had no idea why he'd asked that question. If the answer was going to lead to her saying she was leaving to go back to D.C., he didn't want to hear it.

"I don't quite remember everything, but you could help me with that."

"What can't you remember?"

"I know you proposed to me six years ago, but I'm not sure exactly how you did it. Could you show me?"

Her voice had grown velvety smooth, teasing, yet seductive. And he was not processing fast enough to know where she was going with this. He'd just have to hang on as best he could.

"I don't think I can handle the down-on-the-knee thing."

"You didn't even manage that the first time, and you had a perfectly good knee."

"I thought you didn't remember."

"It's coming back. Slowly. Show me what you did, tell me what you said."

"I asked you to go for a ride with me." He warmed inside, remembering the morning and the nervous anticipation that had left him as awkward as a teenager. "We rode to the top of the same hill where we had breakfast the other morning."

"And you brought a bottle of chilled white wine and real crystal glasses." She crawled up on her knees and feathered his mouth with kisses.

"Hey, wait a minute. I thought this was my memory."

"I was only helping."

He kissed her hard and quick. "Okay, jump in with the kisses any time."

"Tell me what you said, Clint. I want to hear it again. If you remember."

"I remember." Desire awakened inside him, though he had no idea where his body found the energy. Except that Darlene was curled up beside him, her face scrubbed clean, the silky tresses of her hair falling free.

He twisted, ignoring the pain it sent scurrying up his leg, so that he could look into her eyes. The feelings he felt were reflected in their depths. The love he saw there was unmistakable. It took his breath away.

"Say the words, all of them." She touched her fingers to his lips. "I need to hear them tonight."

"I love you, Darlene. I can't promise skies that are always blue, and I can't lay the world at your feet." He was amazed that the speech he'd practiced so long ago was still so fresh in his mind, and at how rapidly his heart was beating as he repeated it now. He swallowed the catch in his voice and went on. "But I promise that I will never stop loving you." He touched his lips to hers, and the kiss rocked his very soul.

He pulled away. The speech was over, but he owed her more. "I made mistakes, Darlene. I pushed you away just like you said, when I couldn't face my own demons. But I kept my promise. I never stopped loving you for a second—not in all the long, lonely six years.''

He kissed her then, the sweetness of her mingling with his breath, the sheer joy of holding her singing in his veins. He didn't pull away until she pushed against his chest with her hands.

''I made a few mistakes myself. I was young and impetuous. When you shut me out, I was sure it was commitment you were afraid of, especially with a woman who was just beginning to discover who she was, a woman who wanted a career.'' She brushed his lips with hers. ''But I'm all grown up now, and I'm waiting for the last line of that proposal.''

He hadn't forgotten. He just hadn't been sure she was ready to hear it. But there was no risk for him, no peril in putting his heart on the line. He'd done that the second she'd dropped back into his life. He took both her hands in his and captured her gaze.

''Will you be my wife?''

A tear fell from the corner of her left eye and rolled down her cheek. Clint kissed it away. ''You don't have to answer until you're ready.''

She pulled her hands from his and locked them around his neck. ''I've fallen in love with you twice, Clint Richards. The first time, it was a giddy roller-coaster ride that left my heart splintered into a million pieces. This time it's passion, so rich and warm that it sears clear to my soul. Both times it was breathtaking and beautiful and touched with magic.''

Tears were streaming down her face now. She wiped them away with the back of her hand. ''Yes, I'll marry you. And this time there's no getting rid of me.''

He gathered her in his arms, and held her close, his heart filled to overflowing. She caught his lips in a kiss of promise, and six years of heartbreak melted away.

Darlene was home to stay.

Epilogue

"Another call for you, Senator McCord." Mary draped her hand over the receiver so the caller wouldn't hear her complaining. "I don't think those reporters are ever going to let you sit down to Christmas dinner. The turkey's going to be dry as jerky if we don't get to it soon."

"Take a message and then put the answering machine back on. I want to talk to Clint and Darlene a minute, and then I promise we'll devour every wonderful dish in sight. Without one interruption from the telephone."

Mary followed her boss's instructions, and hurried back to the kitchen, mumbling just loud enough that they could all hear. "People too busy to eat Christmas dinner are just too busy."

"It looks like the people of America have had their say," Clint said, walking to the hearth to stand next to McCord. "They're yelling for an American hero to lead them into the new millennium. They want you, a man who can do what has to be done."

"No one's more surprised than I. I thought when that story broke, they'd want me tarred and feathered."

"Apparently, the citizens of the country are smarter than we give them credit for," Darlene added.

"Or at least more forgiving." McCord propped a

booted foot on the hearth. "Now we have one more hurdle to clear."

Clint buried his hands in his back pockets. "Another secret?"

"It has been." McCord dropped his gaze to stare at the bricks in the hearth. "I don't know how you feel about this, Clint, but if I run for president, I want my life to be an open book. No secrets. No scandals to leak and hurt the country."

"No illegitimate sons to come out of the woodwork." Bitterness tinged Clint's tone. "You don't have to worry, Senator. Your secret is safe with me."

"No. If I run, I want to tell the whole truth. So, this is your call—*son*."

His voice broke on the word *son*, and Darlene could almost feel the emotion that surged through him. She also knew that Clint had not fully resigned himself to all that the word implied. She stepped between them and linked her fingers with Clint's.

McCord twisted his toe against a brick as if he were smashing an insect. "If you don't want anyone to know I'm your biological father, to know the circumstances of your conception, I'll pull my name from the list of contenders. My first consideration has always been for my family." He finally looked up and made eye contact with Clint. "And you're part of the family now. Actually, you've always been. My will has always stated that when I die, half of the ranch and everything else I own goes to you. The other half goes to Levi."

Clint shifted, turning to look out the window and across a pasture dotted with cattle. "I had a father."

"I know you did." McCord put his hand on Clint's shoulder. Clint stiffened, but didn't pull away. "He was a good man. He was my friend."

"I can't change the past. If you want to admit that I'm your illegitimate son and take your chances with the public's accepting that, I won't stand in the way."

Darlene knew what that concession cost Clint, but she also knew that his love for McCord ran deep. That was why the breach that had developed between them had tortured him so. It would take him time, but he would come around.

"One other thing, Clint. I don't expect an answer tonight, but I'd like for you to consider running my ranch along with yours. There's plenty of room here in the big house for you and Darlene, what with Levi moving to Montana and me in D.C. half the time. Or we can build another house, as big as Darlene wants it. Spread out enough to raise a whole passel of kids. It's up to you, of course. I just thought you should know I'd like to have you here with me. With the family."

Clint slipped an arm around Darlene's shoulder. "I'll think about it." He put out his hand to shake on it, but McCord clapped him on the back.

"That's all I ask. I know you'll do what's right."

"Thanks...Dad."

Darlene blinked back a tear. She hoped she had a lot of sons. Daughters too. They would be born into a wonderful heritage.

"Merry Christmas," Clint whispered, taking her hand as they walked into the dining room to share the McCord Christmas dinner.

"And a happy new century," she whispered back.

It would be, she knew. She'd share it with the man she loved.

*Get ready for heart-pounding romance
and white-knuckle suspense!*

HARLEQUIN®

I N T R I G U E ®

raises the stakes in a new miniseries

★ THE McCORD ★
FAMILY
★ COUNTDOWN ★

The McCord family of Texas is in a desperate race against time!

With a killer on the loose and the clock ticking toward midnight, a daughter will indulge in her passion for her bodyguard; a son will come to terms with his past and help a woman with amnesia find hers; an outsider will do anything to save his unborn child and the woman he loves.

With time as the enemy, only love can save them!

#533 STOLEN MOMENTS
B.J. Daniels
October 1999

#537 MEMORIES AT MIDNIGHT
Joanna Wayne
November 1999

#541 EACH PRECIOUS HOUR
Gayle Wilson
December 1999

Available at your favorite retail outlet.

HARLEQUIN®
Makes any time special ™

Visit us at www.romance.net

HICD

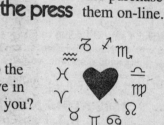

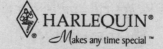